"It sounds more like a family thing."

"I'm sure. Come with us. You can keep an eye on me, see how I'm doing, interacting with CJ. Then later, you can give me more advice."

Tori laughed, the sound like a song in the night. "Oh, so that's it. You want me around to help you improve your relationship with CJ."

"That's my story and I'm sticking to it. Come with us."

"Why do I get the feeling you're after more than parenting advice from me?"

"Wait."

"For what?"

"For this." Connor dared to take her gently by the arms and pull her against him.

And then he kissed her.

Dear Reader,

One thing in life is certain: change. Times are a little tougher in Thunder Canyon, Montana, lately. The boom created by the gold rush a few years ago is over. And Thunder Canyon Resort, which once gave Vail and Aspen a run for their money, is struggling to stay afloat.

Corporate shark and East Coast power player Connor McFarlane has been going through a few changes himself lately. He's in town for the summer to get to know his estranged fifteen-year-old son and make amends with his sister, Melanie. There's also a rumor he's engineering a takeover of Thunder Canyon Resort.

Connor intends to meet his goals this Montana summer and go. Until he meets schoolteacher Tori Jones. A recent bitter divorce has left him wanting nothing to do with love. And he never plans to marry again.

But Tori Jones is a very special woman—just possibly the perfect woman for him.

Happy reading, everyone.

Yours,

Christine Rimmer

McFARLANE'S PERFECT BRIDE

CHRISTINE RIMMER

🖋 *Silhouette*®

S P E C I A L E D I T I O N®

Published by Silhouette Books

America's Publisher of Contemporary Romance

Special thanks and acknowledgment
to Christine Rimmer for her contribution to the
Montana Mavericks: Thunder Canyon Cowboys miniseries.

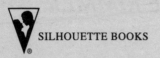 SILHOUETTE BOOKS

ISBN-13: 978-0-373-65535-9

Recycling programs
for this product may
not exist in your area.

McFARLANE'S PERFECT BRIDE

Visit Silhouette Books at www.eHarlequin.com

Printed in U.S.A.

CHRISTINE RIMMER

came to her profession the long way around. Before settling down to write about the magic of romance, she'd been everything from an actress to a salesclerk to a waitress. Now that she's finally found work that suits her perfectly, she insists she never had a problem keeping a job—she was merely gaining "life experience" for her future as a novelist. Christine is grateful not only for the joy she finds in writing, but for what waits when the day's work is through: a man she loves, who loves her right back, and the privilege of watching their children grow and change day to day. She lives with her family in Oklahoma. Visit Christine at www.christinerimmer.com.

For all you teachers out there.
The work you do is the most important work there is.

Chapter One

The doorbell rang just as Tori Jones set the snack tray on the breakfast nook table. "Help yourselves." She gave her star student, Jerilyn Doolin, a fond smile and sent a nod in the direction of Jerilyn's new friend, CJ. "There's juice in the fridge."

Jerilyn pushed her chair back. "Thanks, Ms. Jones."

The doorbell chimed again. "I'll just see who that is." Tori hurried to answer.

She'd made it halfway through her great room to the small foyer when the pounding started. Hard. On the door. The bell rang again, twice, fast. Followed by more pounding. Alarm jangled through her at the loud, frantic sounds. Was there a fire?

"All right, all right. I'm coming, I'm coming…"

She yanked the door wide on a tall, hot-looking guy in designer jeans and high-dollar boots.

Before she could get out a yes-may-I-help-you, the guy growled, "That's my son's skateboard." With a stabbing motion of his index finger, he pointed. Tori peered around the door frame at the skateboard that Jerilyn's friend had left propped against the porch wall. "Do you have my son here?" the stranger demanded.

Have him? Like she'd kidnapped the boy or something? Tori felt her temper rise.

She tamped it down by reminding herself that the angry man in front of her was probably scared to death. And then she spotted the gorgeous, gas-guzzling SUV parked at the curb. Had he been driving up one street and down another looking for a sign of his lost child? Thunder Canyon, Montana, wasn't a big city. But the streets would have to seem endless to a man frantically searching for his missing kid.

"I asked you a question." The man raked his fingers back through thick, expertly cut auburn hair.

Tori schooled her voice to a calmness she didn't feel. "Is your son's name CJ?"

"That's right." The man seemed on the verge of grabbing her and shaking her until she produced the boy. "Is he here?"

"Yes, he is. He's—" With a startled cry, she jumped back as the guy barged into her house.

"Where?" He snarled the word at her. "Take me to him. Now."

"Wait a minute. You can't—"

Oh, but he could. He was already past her, striding boldly into her great room, shouting, "CJ, damn it! CJ!"

Jerilyn and CJ appeared from the kitchen, both wide-eyed. But as soon as CJ caught sight of the furious man, he put on a scowl. "Sheesh, Dad. Chill."

"What is the matter with you?" Mr. Hotshot stopped where he was and started lecturing his son. "I had no clue where you had gotten off to. You know you are not to leave the house without telling Gerda where you're going."

CJ's face flamed. He stared down at the hardwood floor, his shaggy hair falling forward to cover his red cheeks. "Come on, Dad," he muttered. "I was only—"

"And what about your phone? You promised me you wouldn't go off without your phone."

"Like it even works in the canyon." The boy was still talking to the floor.

"Speak up," his father demanded. "I can't hear you."

CJ, who had seemed a normal, reasonably friendly teenager before his dad showed up, clamped his mouth shut now. He refused to even look at his father.

Tori realized she'd been standing there speechless for too long. She needed to calm the father down and diffuse the considerable tension. "Listen, why don't we all go into the kitchen and—"

"No, thanks." CJ's dad cut her off with an absent wave of his hand. "We're going. Come on, CJ. Now." He turned for the door. The boy followed him out, head low, feet dragging.

Tori longed to stop them, to get them to speak civilly to each other, at least, before they took off. But she knew that was only her inner schoolteacher talking. In the end, she had no right to interfere. CJ seemed embarrassed by his dad, but not the least afraid of him. And she couldn't see herself getting between father and son unless there was real cause. Overbearing rudeness just wouldn't cut it as a reason to intervene.

Trailing after his dad, the boy went out into the June sunshine, pulling the door shut behind him. Tori and Jerilyn hardly moved until they heard the engine of that pricey SUV start up outside and drive away.

Jerilyn broke the echoing silence first. "CJ hates his dad." She spoke wistfully. "I don't get that. Yeah, his dad was mad. But at least he cares…"

A low sound of sympathy escaped Tori. Jerilyn's mom had died of cancer the year before. Since then, her father walked around in a daze, emotionally paralyzed with grief. Butch Doolin used to dote on his only child. But not since he lost his wife. Jerilyn had confided in Tori that lately she wondered if her dad even knew she existed anymore.

Tori went to her and smoothed her thick black hair. "How 'bout some cheese, whole-wheat crackers and fresh fruit?"

Jerilyn's wistful expression faded. She giggled. "Ms. Jones, did you ever serve a snack that wasn't healthy?"

"Not a chance." She took the girl by the shoulders and turned her toward the kitchen.

As they sipped organic cranberry juice and nibbled on sliced apples and rennet-free white cheddar, Jerilyn talked about CJ. "I've seen him a couple of times before in the past week, riding his skateboard around Heritage Park. I never thought he'd notice me. But today, he stopped and we started talking…" A dreamy look made her dark eyes shine. "It was so strange, the way we connected, you know? It seemed like we could instantly tell each other everything. I felt so…comfortable with him. And, yeah, he dresses like a skater and he wears his hair long and all, but he's very smart. He's fifteen, same as me. He skipped fourth grade, just like I did."

It was good to hear a little about the boy. Tori'd had no time to ask the pertinent questions before the furious father arrived.

She sipped her juice. "You really like him."

Jerilyn smiled shyly. "I hope maybe I'll see him again. He's going to some expensive boarding school back east in the fall. But even if he stayed here in Thunder Canyon for school, he'd probably end up hanging with the rich, popular kids…"

Tori slid her glass across the table and clinked it with Jerilyn's. "Uh-uh. Don't go there. You have no reason to start beating yourself up. You're every bit as good— and twice as pretty—as any girl at Thunder Canyon High."

Jerilyn wrinkled her nose. "You say that 'cause I'm smart and I understand *Moby Dick* better than most college students."

"I say it 'cause it's true. Your being smart is a bonus." She ate a strawberry. "I have to admit, though. I can't help but love a student who stays on top of the reading list and writes a better essay than I can—and though we didn't have much chance to talk, it definitely seemed to me that CJ liked you."

"You're just saying that to make me feel better."

"Jerilyn." Tori spoke sternly.

"Yes, Ms. Jones?"

"If I say it, I mean it."

"Yes, Ms. Jones." Jerilyn sighed. "You *really* think he likes me?"

"I do. I really do. And he seemed like a nice boy."

"I'm so glad you liked him." Jerilyn beamed.

Too bad his dad's such a complete jerk, Tori thought, but didn't say.

"Tall, good-looking, auburn-haired, buttoned-down. Obviously rich. Pushy. And rude?" asked Allaire Traub, who was Tori's dearest friend.

Tori took the fruit and cheese tray from earlier that day out of the fridge and pulled off the plastic wrap. "That's him."

Allaire's two-year-old, Alex, who sat on her lap, started chanting in a singsong. "Rude, rude, rude, rude…"

"Shh," Allaire chided. She kissed his dark brown baby curls. Tori set the tray on the table and Allaire gave Alex a slice of apple.

"Apple. Yum," said the little boy.

Tori slid into the chair opposite her friend. "So…you know him?"

"Well, I know *of* him." Allaire rescued Alex's sippy cup just as he was about to knock it to the floor. She kissed his cheek and commanded adoringly, "Eat your apple and sit still."

"Apple, apple, apple, apple." The little boy giggled. And then he stuck the slice of apple in his mouth. He was quiet. For the moment.

Tori prompted, "And his name is…?"

Allaire frowned. "Who?"

"Mr. Buttoned-down, Pushy and Rude?"

"Oh. Right. He's Connor McFarlane, Melanie Chilton's brother."

Tori put her hands to her cheeks. "Of course. I should

have known." Melanie McFarlane had come to town three years ago determined to prove herself to her rich, snobby family. She'd ended up opening a guest ranch and marrying a local rancher, Russ Chilton. "Connor McFarlane. He runs the family empire, right?"

Allaire nodded. "McFarlane House Hotels." She passed her son an orange wedge. "He's here for the summer, with his son, Connor Jr."

"Aka, CJ."

"That's right." Allaire gave Alex his sippy cup—then took it away when he started to pound it on the edge of the table.

"I thought Melanie and her brother didn't get along."

"Rumor is they're trying, you know? Connor's been taken down a peg since the economy dipped. The way I heard it, McFarlane House had to pull back. A serious retrenchment. They closed a few hotels. The company is holding strong now, but not growing the way it was. And Connor's personal fortune took a serious hit, though I understand he's still a long way from the poorhouse. His wife dumped him. And CJ, formerly the perfect son, has been acting out. Melanie suggested that her brother and CJ come to Montana for the summer. Connor's renting one of those big houses in New Town that all the newcomers built—and then tried to unload when the bottom fell out."

In spite of herself, Tori felt sympathy rising. "His wife divorced him?"

Allaire nodded. "Pretty much out of nowhere, apparently. Story goes that she met someone richer."

Tori shook her head. "How do you *know* all this stuff?"

Allaire lifted a delicate, gold-dusted eyebrow. "To many, I may seem merely a deceptively fragile-looking über-talented art teacher and loving wife and mother. But I also have my finger on the pulse of Thunder Canyon."

"Because you're married to DJ," Tori said with a chuckle.

Allaire shrugged. "You know my husband. He makes it his business to keep an eye on the movers and shakers. Even if they're supposedly only visiting for the summer."

DJ Traub ran a successful chain of mid-priced restaurants with locations all over the western states. When he returned to town to stay a few years ago, he'd opened a DJ's Rib Shack on-site at the sprawling, upscale Thunder Canyon Resort, which covered most of nearby Thunder Mountain. The resort gave Vail and Aspen a run for the money—or it had until the financial downturn. DJ knew everybody *and* what they were up to.

Alex waved his chewed orange rind. "DJ, DJ, that's my daddy!"

"Oh, yes, he is." Allaire hugged him close and said to Tori, "You *are* coming to the barbecue up at the resort Saturday, right?"

"Wouldn't miss it. I thought I'd bring Jerilyn."

"Great. She'll like that. It's really good of you to look out for her."

"It's no hardship. She's a joy to have around."

Allaire gazed at Tori fondly. "She reminds you of yourself."

"A little, maybe." Tori had lost her mom when she was thirteen. Her dad had been really out of it for a while, trying to deal with the loss.

"And *your* dad got better, eventually."

"Yes, he did." Now she had a stepmother she loved and three half brothers ages ten, six and three.

"So there's hope that Butch Doolin will pull it together."

Tori was trying to think of something positive to say about Jerilyn's dad when Alex started pounding his little fist in the table. "More juice," the toddler commanded. Allaire put the cup in his chubby hand. This time, he actually drank from it. "Here, Mommy." He gave the cup back. "I tired." He set his apple core on the table and snuggled back into his mother's arms. In seconds, he was fast asleep.

"Amazing," said Tori with a doting smile.

Allaire made a tender sound of agreement as she smoothed his springy curls. Softly, so as not to wake him, she spoke of the small family reunion she and DJ were hosting out at their ranch that weekend. A couple of Traub cousins, wealthy ones, were coming up from Texas for the event. They would all be at the Rib Shack for the barbecue Saturday.

Tori still had Connor McFarlane on her mind. She asked in a near-whisper, "What do you mean, Connor's 'supposedly' only visiting for the summer?"

Allaire set the sippy cup on the table. "Well, DJ says Connor's been at the resort a lot. Chatting people up, nosing around. And Grant told DJ that Connor's had dinner with Caleb Douglas out at the Douglas Ranch." Caleb Douglas was co-owner of the resort. Grant Clifton managed the place, with help from Riley Douglas, Caleb's son.

Tori frowned. "A takeover? I knew the resort was

struggling lately. But would Caleb do that? The resort is his pride and joy."

"Money's short. Even the Douglases need to tighten their belts."

"But I mean, would Caleb really sell?"

Allaire made a noncommittal noise in her throat. "Can't say for sure. But *something's* going on."

"You're going," Connor said flatly. "And we're late."

CJ didn't spare him so much as a glance. He was busy manipulating the black controller of his Xbox 360 Elite, wearing a headset so he could talk to whomever he was playing with online—and also shut his father out. On the flatscreen that took up half a wall of his bedroom, soldiers in WWII Army gear battled the Germans somewhere in a burned-out city in France. A tank lurched over rubble and belched fire as a building exploded and a couple of hapless Germans went flying in the air, faces contorted with fear.

Connor stood by the bed. His blood pressure had to be spiking. He wanted to shout, *What the hell have you done with my son?* He hardly knew this shaggy-looking, angry, sulky kid. The CJ he knew gazed at him with worshipful eyes and only wanted a chance to spend a little time with his busy, successful dad.

I will not shout. I will not rip those headphones off of his head.

Connor fisted his hands and counted to ten. And then he grabbed the TV remote off the bed and pointed it at the flatscreen.

The screen went black.

CJ slanted him a venomous look. "Turn it back on. Now."

Connor did nothing of the sort. With a calmness he didn't feel, he reached out and gently pulled the headset from CJ's ears. "I told you we were going to the big summer kickoff barbecue." The barbecue, at DJ's Rib Shack up at the resort, presented a useful opportunity to get more face time with people he needed to know better—family and otherwise. "Your Aunt Melanie and Uncle Russ are going. Ryan, too." Ryan Chilton, Russ's son from his first marriage, was thirteen.

CJ groaned and tossed the controller aside. "I'm not babysitting Ryan."

"No one said anything about babysitting. You will, however, behave in a civilized manner and treat your aunt and her family with respect."

"I hate that kind of crap. 'Big summer kickoff barbecue.'" He chanted the words in an angry singsong. "Big whoop."

Again, Connor reminded himself that shouting and threats had so far gotten him nowhere. He spoke with deadly mildness. "Fine. Stay home if you like. Stay home all summer. In this room. With no electronics."

CJ blinked. "You would *ground* me forever for missing some dumb barbecue?"

"Try me."

CJ glared at him. Connor stared steadily back.

And then, at last, CJ put down the remote. "Fine. Let's go." He jumped to his feet and headed for the door in his sloppy skater gear, which included ripped-out, sagging jeans, a wrinkled plaid shirt over a T-shirt that had seen better days. And dirty old-school tennis shoes with the laces undone.

Connor reminded himself that the barbecue was casual and he didn't have time for a wardrobe battle.

CJ stopped in the doorway and turned with a glare. "Well? You coming or not?"

Connor straightened his sport jacket and gave a brisk nod. "Absolutely. I am right behind you."

The resort was packed. People spilled out of the Rib Shack and filled up the huge central lobby of the main clubhouse.

Connor spotted Melanie, Russ and Ryan over by the lobby's natural-stone fireplace, which was on a grand scale, like the rest of the clubhouse. Big enough to roast a couple of steers inside and still have room for an elk or three.

He hooked an arm around CJ's shoulders to keep him from slipping off and worked his way through the crowd, spreading greetings as he went. Melanie saw him just before he reached her. She smiled and waved, her sleek red hair shining in the afternoon sun that beamed down from the skylights three stories overhead and flooded in the soaring wall of windows with its amazing view of the white-capped peak of Thunder Mountain.

She was a fine woman, his sister. And forgiving. All those years he'd looked down on her. And still, she'd welcomed him to her new hometown and seemed to want only to let bygones be bygones. She made him feel humble, an emotion with which he'd had no relationship until recently.

Russ gave him a cool nod. Ryan's face split in a happy grin at the sight of his older cousin.

CJ squirmed a little under Connor's firm grip and said loudly, "Well, we're here. Can we eat?"

Ryan nodded eagerly. "In the Rib Shack. Come on, I'll show you…"

Connor hesitated to let go of his son. "Stay in the building."

"Sheesh, Dad. Awright, awright."

"Stay with Ryan."

"I will, I will."

Melanie caught his eye. "I'm sure they'll be fine."

Russ spoke to Ryan. "Get us a table if you can."

"We will, Dad. Come on, CJ." He bounded off through the crowd, headed for the Rib Shack. CJ followed, kind of shuffling along. Watching them go, Connor actually found himself envying Russ his happy, upbeat son.

Russ was watching the boys, too. "Job's still open," he said in that cryptic way he had.

The job in question was for CJ. Russ and Melanie had offered to hire him part-time for the summer, to work at Melanie's guest ranch, the Hopping H. Russ thought a few hours a day mucking out stables or doing dishes in the ranch house would be good for him.

When Russ had made the initial offer, Connor had turned him down flat. The McFarlane offspring did not do dishes or clean up horse manure. Plus, at that point, Connor had still nurtured the fond hope that CJ might spend his summer catching up on his schoolwork. Just weeks before, the boy had almost been booted out of his expensive New York boarding school due to his suddenly plummeting grades.

However, in the eleven days they'd been in Thunder Canyon, Connor had not seen his son so much as pick up a book. CJ rode his skateboard around town, disappearing for hours at a time, worrying Connor half out of his mind. When he wasn't vanishing into thin air, he sat in his room and played video games.

Connor had started to wonder if he should reconsider Russ's job offer. He asked ruefully, "Mind if I think it over a little?"

Russ and Melanie shared a glance. And Russ answered in a neutral tone. "Take your time. The job will be there if you want him to have it."

A big hand clapped Connor on the back. "Glad you came. Good to see you."

He turned and greeted Caleb Douglas and his wife, Adele. Silver-haired with cool green eyes, Caleb had suffered poor health in recent years. He still had a booming voice and a hearty manner, but Connor could see the weariness in his face, the deep lines around his eyes. He was half owner of the resort, which meant he would feel duty-bound to show up for big events like this one.

But his heart wasn't in it anymore. And times were tougher than they had been. Caleb could be convinced to sell. And Connor's extensive research into the matter had led him to believe that Caleb's silent partner would go along with whatever Caleb decided.

Yeah, Caleb would sell. Hopefully, before the summer was out.

And for a very reasonable price.

Caleb made small talk for a minute or two, then stepped in close to Connor while Adele chatted up Melanie and Russ.

The older man spoke low so only Connor could hear.

"Come on out to the ranch again. We'll…talk some more."

"I'd like that." Connor smiled.

"Excellent—but next week's no good. Adele's dragging me to Hawaii." Caleb grunted. "Lately Adele's got some idea that we should travel more. But how about a week from Monday? Dinner, seven-thirty?"

"I'll be there, thanks."

A minute or two later, Caleb and his wife moved on.

Next, Grant Clifton appeared with his pretty wife, Stephanie, and a Clifton cousin, Beauregard, who was known as Bo.

Bo was good-looking and talkative, a rancher by trade—and a salesman by nature. "I think we need some fresh ideas in this old town. And that's why I'm running for mayor."

Grant laughed. "Come on, Bo. Against Arthur?"

"Arthur Swinton is a staunch conservative," Melanie explained for Connor's benefit.

Russ said, "Been in town politics for years."

Grant added, "Arthur's on the city council and he's running for mayor. It's pretty much a given he's going to win."

Bo laughed. "Nothing's a given, cousin."

Russ suggested dryly, "Don't forget death and taxes."

"You're right," agreed Bo. "And for the sales tax we pay around here, we should get more for our money." Bo went on to explain in detail all the projects he planned to fight for when he won the election.

When Grant and Stephanie finally dragged Bo away, Melanie suggested they start moving in the general direction of the Rib Shack. Connor turned for the wide arch that led through to the restaurant and almost ran into the woman standing behind him.

Slim, with short, wispy, strawberry-blond hair, the woman wore a snug summer dress splashed with vivid pink flowers. He couldn't see her face. She was turned the other way.

"Tori, hey," said Melanie, who apparently knew her.

The woman turned to smile at his sister. But the smile faded when she saw him. She gazed up at him warily, through big, bright hazel eyes.

He stifled a groan of embarrassment as he remembered where he'd seen her before.

Chapter Two

Connor felt like a jerk.

Probably because he'd behaved like one the other day.

"Hello," the woman named Tori said coolly.

Jones, he thought, scouring his brain for the information CJ had reluctantly given up when Connor had grilled him after he got the kid home on Thursday. Her name was Tori Jones and she taught English at the high school. "How are you?" he asked, for lack of anything more original to say.

"Just fine, thank you." And then, finally, she did smile—over his shoulder, at Melanie. "Hey." She even smiled at Russ. And she had that teenage girl with her, the one CJ liked, whose name was Jerilyn.

The girl said, "Hi, Mr. McFarlane."

He cleared his throat. "Uh. Hi, Jerilyn."

"Is, um, CJ here, too?" Her pretty face was open, guileless. And heartbreakingly hopeful.

His sister said, "Ah. So you've met my big brother?"

"Yes, we have," Tori Jones said sweetly. "Just the other day, as a matter of fact."

Connor told the dark-haired girl, "CJ's in the restaurant, with Ryan."

And Melanie said, "Why don't you two join us? We were just going in to eat."

Jerilyn turned her hopeful gaze on the English teacher.

After a moment, Tori nodded. "Sure. Why not?"

So they all went together, easing their way through the crowd toward the packed Rib Shack.

As it turned out, Ryan and CJ had actually managed to save three chairs. CJ jumped up at the sight of Jerilyn. "Jerilyn! Hi." Suddenly he was only too eager to scout out a couple more seats for the dark-haired girl and her teacher.

They went through the serving line and loaded their plates with ribs, barbecued chicken, fat white rolls and coleslaw. Back at the table, CJ worked it so that Jerilyn sat next to him. The girl seemed to glow with pleasure at CJ's attention. And CJ behaved almost like his old self, suddenly—smiling and happy, his face animated as he and the girl whispered together.

Connor ended up with Melanie on one side and Tori Jones on the other. Through the meal, his sister and Tori talked around him—about the barbecue and what a success it was, about the resort and how nice it was to see it packed full of people again.

Since Russ had bought the first beers for the four

adults, Connor did his bit and went over to the bar to get a second round. He eased in next to a blonde woman, sitting alone, nursing a white wine.

She smiled and leaned close to him. "I'm Erin. Erin Castro."

Was she coming on to him?

He decided she wasn't. There was no breathless smile, no fluttering eyelashes. Probably just being friendly. He gave her offered hand a quick shake. "Connor McFarlane."

She seemed to study his face intently. "No relation to the Traubs, the Cliftons or the Cateses?" She had named the town's three major families.

He laughed. "No, but they're thick on the ground around here."

"So I've been told."

He paid the bartender, gathered up the four beers by their necks and headed back to the table, forgetting about the woman named Erin as soon as he turned away from her. Mostly, he was thinking about Tori Jones.

Thinking that he liked the cute spray of freckles across her nose and those big hazel eyes. Thinking that he owed her an apology for his behavior on Thursday. After all, he *was* trying to be a better man. And one of the things a better man did was to say he was sorry when an apology was called for.

Sometimes trying to be a better man could be a real pain in the ass.

At the table, he took the chair next to her again and set one of the beers in front of her. "Here you go."

She met his eyes. "Thanks."

"My pleasure." Holding her gaze, he tried a smile.

She didn't smile back. And yet somehow that look they shared went on far too long.

She glanced away first.

He passed fresh ones down the table to Melanie and Russ and tried to think of how he could smoothly suggest that the schoolteacher give him a moment alone.

Smoothly. That was the key. But for some reason, he didn't feel especially smooth. And that really bugged him. He ran a hotel chain, for pity's sake. It was part of his job to be smooth when a situation required it.

After the meal, which included red velvet cake and coffee for dessert, DJ Traub got up with a microphone and thanked everyone for coming to his annual summer kickoff barbecue. He introduced his visiting Texas cousins, Dillon and Corey, after which he announced there would be dancing out on the patio. Everyone applauded as DJ left the mike.

CJ stood and pulled back Jerilyn's chair for her.

Connor snapped to attention. "What's up?"

His son stiffened. But then Jerilyn gave CJ a gentle look. That was all it took. CJ actually spoke in civil tone. "We were just going to hang around out in the lobby area."

"If that's all right," Jerilyn added, stars in her dark eyes.

"Just the lobby," Connor warned.

CJ nodded.

Jerilyn promised, "Just the lobby, Mr. McFarlane. By the big fireplace."

"All right."

The girl turned her warm smile on Ryan. "Come with us," she offered softly. CJ looked a little sulky about that, but he didn't object.

"Sure." Ryan, his face lit up like a Christmas tree, jumped to his feet and bounced off in the wake of the two older kids.

"She's a lovely girl," said Melanie.

On his other side, Tori made a soft noise of agreement.

Out on the patio, the band DJ had hired struck up a country song. Russ took Melanie's hand and got up. "'Scuse me while I dance with my beautiful wife."

Melanie rose. "We'll be back." Russ put his arm around her.

Connor watched them make their way through the thicket of tables to the open patio doors, leaving him alone with the cute schoolteacher and his chance to make amends.

How to begin?

He had no clue. He felt awkward, tongue-tied as a kid with his first crush. Which was pretty ridiculous, really. He did not have a crush on Tori Jones. He'd just been put through the wringer with the divorce and the last thing he needed was another relationship.

Deeply annoyed with himself for feeling nervous, and for finding the schoolteacher much too attractive, he stared out through the open doors at the patio and the couples dancing there and started thinking about CJ.

And the girl, Jerilyn.

Jerilyn seemed like a kind-hearted person. And she was certainly polite and respectful of adults. But still, he'd better ask around, find out for certain she was really okay.

Being a full-time father was a challenge. You couldn't just tell a kid to get with the program or get out, like you could an employee. The cold fact was that Connor's life had been a damn sight simpler before the divorce, when CJ had been Jennifer's responsibility and Connor was free to wheel and deal around the clock.

It had been Jennifer's idea that he should take the boy to live with him for the summer, leaving her free to float around the Mediterranean on a luxury yacht with her new shipping magnate boyfriend. Connor might have refused. But he had felt obligated to spend some time with his son. Yes, it was probably too little too late. But CJ really needed guidance now and Connor was determined to try to provide it.

Beside him, the schoolteacher shifted in her chair. The movement reminded him that he couldn't avoid facing her forever—and that to keep staring off into space while she was sitting right next to him was borderline rude.

He turned to her.

Those hazel eyes were waiting. A slight, knowing smile tipped the corners of her mouth and he realized she'd been watching him.

"What?" he demanded, knowing he sounded as surly as CJ did most of the time.

She only shrugged, a delicate movement of one slim shoulder.

"All right," he said. "It's like this. I've been trying to figure out how to tell you I'm sorry for my behavior Thursday afternoon. I wanted to be smooth about it, you know?"

Damn. What was the matter with him? Had he actually just said out loud that he wanted to be smooth?

Apparently, he had, because she repeated, "Smooth, huh?"

"You're grinning," he accused.

She tipped her head to the side. "You know, you're kind of cute when you're embarrassed."

He narrowed his eyes at her. "A McFarlane is never cute and very rarely embarrassed."

She laughed then, a full-throated, musical sound.

He heard himself say, "You've got a great laugh."

Her laughter faded as quickly as it had come. She tipped her strawberry-blond head the other way and said softly, "Your apology is accepted. I know you must have been worried sick."

He answered honestly, "Yeah. I was." And then he actually confessed, "Sometimes, lately, I wonder where my son went—and I don't only mean when he disappears on his skateboard and I don't know where to find him."

"Teenagers can be a challenge."

"It's more than that. You should have known him before…" He let the sentence die unfinished. This woman did not need to hear about his broken marriage.

"It will work out," she said. "Just give it time."

He chuckled low. "Is that a promise?"

"Let's call it a professional assessment. I deal with kids his age nine months out of the year and I can spot the ones who are just going through a tough phase. CJ's one of those."

"You think so?"

"I do. And it's good that you're spending time with him."

"I hope you're right. He mostly behaves like he wishes I would get lost and stay that way."

"Don't believe that. He needs you. Maybe he can't— or doesn't know how to—show you. But it matters to him, that you're around and you care."

Another long moment passed. He looked into those big eyes and she gazed back at him. Finally, he said, "Thanks. I appreciate a little reassurance."

"Anytime."

He leaned a little closer to her, got a whiff of her fresh, citrusy perfume. And it suddenly occurred to him that she would be the one to tell him all about Jerilyn. And he did need to know more about the girl, since CJ seemed so gone on her. "I've got a great idea."

The hazel eyes widened. "You do?"

"Yeah. Dinner. You and me. This coming Friday."

She seemed to realize she'd let him get too close and sat back away from him. "Oh. No, really—"

"Yeah. Really. I promise not to yell or say rude things."

"Bad idea. Seriously. Bad."

"What's bad about it?"

She considered for a moment. "Okay, *bad* isn't the right word. I just don't think it's a *good* idea."

"Why not?"

"Call it…instinct."

He laughed. "Your instincts tell you not to go out with me?"

"Yeah. They do."

Should he have been discouraged? He wasn't. He saw the flush of color on her smooth cheeks and knew he could change her mind. "Come on. Take a chance. Friday night, the Gallatin Room right here at the resort. I've heard the food's pretty good."

She laughed again, a softer laugh than the one before, but no less warm, no less musical. "You high-powered types don't take no for an answer."

"So say yes."

Her gaze slid away—and then came back to meet his.

He pressed the advantage. "It's only dinner. What can it hurt?"

Something happened in her eyes. A decision. In his favor. "Good point." She gave him a nod.

"A yes," he said, and felt absurdly triumphant. "You just said yes."

Her gaze dropped to his mouth and then shifted up again, to his eyes. "You remember where I live?"

"I'll never forget."

"Seven-thirty."

"I'll be there."

"You're going out with Connor McFarlane?" Allaire asked in complete disbelief. "Tell me you're joking." She leaned close across the lacy tablecloth. It was Monday at noon. They were having their regular girls-only lunch at the Tottering Teapot on Main Street. DJ was home with Alex so Allaire could have a little time for herself.

The Teapot was famous for really good vegetarian sandwiches and an endless variety of teas, both caffeinated and herbal. All the tables had lace cloths and the food was served on mismatched thrift-store china. Not many men in town ate at the Teapot, but the women loved it.

"Not joking. I'm having dinner with him Friday night." Tori kept her voice low. No reason everyone and their sister needed to hear this conversation.

Allaire demanded, "Why ask for trouble?"

"Because I kind of like him. He can be really charming when he's not terrified something's happened to his son."

"He's a shark. He's trying to take over the resort."

"It's just a rumor. You said so yourself."

"Watch. Wait. You'll see it's more that a rumor."

"Doesn't matter. I like him and I'm going out with him—and will you stop? It's only a date. Not a lifetime commitment."

Allaire pursed her lips in an expression of serious distaste. "You like him a *lot*. I can see it in your eyes."

"In my eyes? Oh, please."

Allaire leaned even closer. "Yep. Right there." She aimed her index and middle fingers directly at Tori and sighted down them. "I can see it. You've got a thing for Mr. Bigshot McFarlane."

Tori waved a hand. "Stop worrying. I'll have a nice dinner and some good conversation. That's all, nothing more."

Allaire made a scoffing sound, but had to quell the rest of the lecture because Haley Anderson came in. In her mid-twenties, Haley went to college part-time and worked at the Hitching Post down the street, a local bar and also a town landmark. She spotted them and Tori waved her over.

"Good news." Haley was beaming. As a rule, she wasn't the beaming type. She'd had a rough time of it, raising her two younger siblings after their parents died. But today, her smile lit up the whole restaurant.

Allaire guessed, "You found a place."

Haley beamed wider. "The price is right and it's just down the street."

Tori thought she knew where. "That vacant storefront down the block from the Hitching Post?"

"That's the one. I met with the property manager, made an offer that's a little lower than what they're asking."

"And?"

"The owner's not in town. The property manager will consult with him and I should get my answer in the next few weeks." Haley hugged herself. "I can just feel it, you know? This is it."

Haley Anderson had a dream. Her dream was called ROOTS. It was to be a sort of Outward Bound/Big Brother organization to help troubled teens. Getting the storefront would mean she had a home base from which to launch the program.

She asked Allaire, "Did you talk with the principal?" She meant at the high school.

Allaire nodded. "He said to bring him a proposal when you're all set up. He really can't do much until then. You should definitely be able to put up flyers around the school, though. I mean, once you're up and running and can show what you're offering."

"Of course. I understand." Haley gave a nervous laugh. "I guess I'm kind of getting ahead of myself."

Tori reached over and squeezed her hand. "It's good to think ahead. And it's a fine project, an important one."

"We'll help all we can," Allaire promised.

Haley went on beaming. "I knew I could count on you two."

The little bell over the door chimed again. It was Melanie Chilton. Ignoring Tori's warning look, Allaire waved her over.

"Join us." Allaire gave Connor's sister a big, sweet smile.

"Only for a minute." Melanie slid in next to Tori. "I've got to get back to the Hopping H." The waitress appeared. They all ordered, with Melanie asking for hers to go. When the waitress left, Melanie asked Allaire, "So how was the weekend reunion?"

"The *mini* reunion," Allaire corrected. "Just the local Traubs and Corey and Dillon. It went great. Both of DJ's cousins say they'll be back in town soon."

"Tell DJ we loved the barbecue. We had a wonderful time."

"So I heard," said Allaire, sending a meaningful look Tori's way.

Melanie glanced at Tori and then back at Allaire. "Okay. What am I not picking up on here?"

Allaire gave an airy wave of her hand. "Oh, nothing."

Tori glared at her, mostly in fun. "You are impossible."

Now Allaire was grinning. "So I've been told."

"What's going on?" Haley demanded.

Tori realized it was kind of silly to try to keep the date with Connor to herself. Everyone in town would know anyway, after she showed up at the resort with him on Friday night. "Connor asked me out to dinner. I said yes. It's not a big deal, but Allaire is trying to make it one."

Melanie blinked. And then she grinned. "I thought there was something going on with you two."

Tori frowned. Everyone seemed to know something she didn't. "You did?"

Haley asked Melanie, "Connor. That's your brother, right?"

Melanie nodded and told Haley what Tori and Allaire

already knew. "He's in town for the summer." And then she lowered her voice so only their table could hear. "He's always been…difficult to get along with, at least, for me. He and my father looked down on me. No matter how hard I worked, I was never good enough, never *man* enough, to be an equal partner in McFarlane House Hotels. But Connor's been surprising me lately. He's different, since his divorce, since he and our father had to sell a couple of failing locations, including the new Atlanta hotel, just to stay afloat."

"You're saying you believe Connor's changed?" asked Allaire, sounding annoyingly doubtful.

"I do," said Melanie. "Or at least, he's not nearly as overbearing as he used to be. Now and then, in the past few days, I even get the feeling he's actually listening to me. And to Russ." And then she chuckled wryly. "My father, though. Donovan McFarlane is a man who'll never change."

"Thunder Canyon, Montana," Donovan McFarlane growled in disgust. "It's a black hole, Connor, and you know it."

Connor reminded himself to breathe slowly and evenly. He ordered his fingers to hold the phone more loosely. "I can get a good deal on the resort. But I need a little time to work on Caleb Douglas, to show him how the best decision for him is to sell."

"McFarlane House does not need a resort in some tiny Montana town. I've seen the numbers on that location. They're not good, trending down."

"Everything's trending down lately." *Even McFarlane House,* Connor thought. "Once we're in charge, we'll start making the necessary changes to get the resort in the black again. We'll cut back, at first, focus on the strongest services, get rid of any staff that isn't ready to—"

"Honestly, I don't know what's gotten into you lately, but I don't like it. First your sister, and now you. Throwing over your life work, your *heritage*."

"Dad. I'm not throwing anything over."

As usual, Donovan wasn't listening "—your sister with her ridiculous dude ranch, you with your sudden burning need to buy that failing resort."

"The Hopping H is doing very well, thanks, Dad. And we agreed that the resort could work for us."

"I agreed to no such thing. I do not care in the least about that resort. I want you back here in Philadelphia right away. I need you here." It was a bald-faced lie. Donovan McFarlane could run the McFarlane House corporate office with one hand tied behind his back and a bag over his head.

"I'll be there next week for the monthly—"

"Not next week. Now. You're welcome to stay with us until you can find another house. Your mother would be only too happy to have you nearby again. Why you had to give Jennifer *your* house is beyond me."

"It was her house, too, Dad."

"What about the prenup? We both know what that prenup said. She had no right to that house. And then she went and sold it, anyway."

"Dad, let's not rehash all this again."

"All right. Come home. You could have at least kept that condo."

"Dad. We discussed this. I sold the condo because when I come back in the fall, I'm going to find another house."

"I've reevaluated and I want—"

"Well, I haven't. Except for the specific meetings and catch-up visits we agreed on two weeks ago, I'm here in Thunder Canyon for the summer with my son."

There was a silence on the other end of the line. A deadly one. Finally, Donovan said, "You could just send Connor Jr. back to school. A summer without distractions, time to focus on his studies. Do the boy a world of good."

"Dad."

"Ahem. What is it?"

"I'm spending the summer here in Thunder Canyon and so is CJ. End of discussion."

"You're very stubborn. You don't get that from me."

Connor almost laughed. It would have been a sound with zero humor in it. "I have to go now, Dad. See you next week." Connor disconnected the call before his father could start issuing more orders.

And then he just stood there, in the study of his rented house, staring blindly out the window at the snowcapped peak of Thunder Mountain in the distance. There had been a time, not that long ago, when he and his dad saw eye to eye on just about every issue.

But now, whenever he talked to Donovan, he hung up wanting to put his fist through a wall. Donovan just didn't get it. Times were changing and a man either swam with the tide or drowned.

Sometimes Connor thought he was a survivor, that he really was changing, working his way toward a better life for himself and the son he'd neglected for too long.

And sometimes he knew he was kidding himself, that

he was actually drowning, going under for the third time and still telling himself he had both feet firmly planted on solid ground.

Chapter Three

"Roses." The schoolteacher looked up at him through those amazing hazel eyes. "You actually brought flowers."

He blinked. "What? That's bad?"

"No, of course not. It's lovely."

He handed them over.

"Thank you." She said it softly. She seemed to mean it. "I should put them in water, huh?"

"Good idea."

She stepped back from the doorway. "Come on in."

So he followed her, admiring the view of her trim backside in a slim-fitting red dress as she led the way through a comfortable-looking great room, back to an open kitchen with turquoise-blue walls and old-fashioned counters of white ceramic tile.

She opened a cupboard by the sink and pointed at

the top shelf. "See that square vase? Could you reach it
for me?"

He got it down and she filled it with water and put the
roses in it, tugging at them this way and that until she
had them arranged to her satisfaction. "So pretty…"

He completely agreed, though it wasn't precisely the
flowers he was looking at.

She slanted him a look. "Want a drink? I have a variety of organic juices. And I think I have an old bottle of
vodka around here somewhere…a screwdriver. I could
make you one of those." She looked so pleased with
herself, he almost said yes, just to stand in her turquoise
kitchen and watch her bustling around, mixing the drink
for him.

Then again… "I'm not really a screwdriver kind of
guy."

"Well, okay." She carried the vase over to the breakfast nook and put it in the center of the table. "Ta-da.
Looks beautiful."

"Yes, it does."

"You ready?"

"After you."

Tori loved the Gallatin Room. She'd only been there a
few times, once before on a date and also for a couple of
parties. It was the best restaurant at the resort—really, in
all of Thunder Canyon—and had a beautiful view of tall,
majestic evergreens and the top of Thunder Mountain. It
also had a massive stone fireplace, one that wasn't quite
as large as the one in the main lobby. But impressive,
nonetheless.

The host led them to a really good table, by the fireplace, with a view of the mountain and the spectacular

sky, shot now with orange and gold as the sun set. A waiter came to take their drink orders. Connor ordered Scotch, the really good kind that was older than Tori. She asked for a glass of white wine.

The drinks appeared instantly. They sat and sipped and watched the sunset.

She said what she was thinking. "I love this restaurant."

His dark eyes made a quick scan of the beautiful room. "It's slow for a Friday evening, don't you think?"

She shrugged. "I guess."

"The Scotch is perfect. And the service so far is excellent. It'll be interesting to see how good the food is. As a rule, it's the first thing to slip."

"Uh, slip?"

He sipped his Scotch slowly. "When traffic declines."

She knew what he meant, but still she teased, "Traffic?"

He set down his glass and regarded her lazily. "When business slows down."

She stared at his fingers, which were still wrapped around the crystal glass. They were very nice fingers. Long. Lean. Strong-looking. "Hotelier to the core, huh?"

He didn't deny it. On the contrary, he gave her a rueful smile as he turned his crystal glass and stared down at the amber liquid inside. "I think it's in the blood. My father would certainly say it is."

She suddenly craved total honesty—no matter how unwise. "Your sister says your father's overbearing. And that he'll never change."

"Melanie's become way too frank in the past couple of years."

"I really like frankness in a person. I also heard you're in town to buy out this resort, after which you'll change everything around and fire half the staff."

"Who said that?" His voice was flat.

"It doesn't matter. Is it true?"

"Don't believe every rumor you hear." He studied her—a long, considering look.

"You're not going to answer my question, are you?" She sipped her wine again, set the glass down. "Never mind. I think you *are* in town to buy this resort. Feel free to tell me I'm wrong."

He staunchly refused to confirm or deny her suspicions. "I'm here to spend time getting to know my sister and her family. And above all, for my son. I've neglected CJ for much too long. I'm hoping it's not too late to heal the breach between us."

She believed he was telling the truth about his son. "It's not too late," she said softly. "It's never too late."

Those dark eyes went soft—but only for a split second. And then they were cool and watchful again. "You're an optimist."

"And proud of it." She picked up the leather-bound menu and set it back down without opening it. "It matters, Connor. That you care about your son, that you *show* him you care. And I admire you for figuring out that you need to spend time with him, no matter how long it took you to realize that."

His gaze was locked hard on hers. "I didn't figure it out. Not by myself, anyway. If my ex-wife hadn't demanded that I take him for the summer, I wouldn't have."

"But you did take him. You could have simply refused."

He almost smiled. "You insist on making me seem a better man than I am."

"Hey." She raised her glass to him. "Gives you something to live up to."

He did smile then. And he picked up his menu and opened it to study the offerings within. She opened hers, too.

The waiter appeared when they set their menus down again. They ordered. Connor asked for a bottle of cabernet to go with the meal.

The wine steward hustled over to confer with Connor. Once the choice was made, the wine had to be tasted. Connor nodded his approval. The waiter served them each a glass. He left the bottle, wrapped in a white cloth, within easy reach.

The food came—appetizers, salads and then the main course. Connor had prime rib, she had the trout. Tori found it all delicious, every last bite. If the quality was going downhill, she couldn't tell.

He asked her about her childhood. She told him of her mother's early death and her father's extended depression following the loss.

"Must have been a hard time."

"It was. But we got through it." She spoke of her half brothers and her stepmother. "My dad's happy now. It all worked out."

"What does your dad do?"

"He's a psychiatrist in Denver. Nowadays he does a lot of pro bono work, helping people deal with grief after the loss of a loved one."

"He would be the one to understand what they're going through, huh?"

"Yes. He understands."

"You admire him."

"I do. Very much."

"You were raised in…?"

"Denver, mostly. I moved here about three years ago."

"And you love it."

"Yep. I plan to live in Thunder Canyon till I'm old and gray."

Eventually, the talk got back around to CJ. He said, "My brother-in-law wants CJ to go to work part-time at the Hopping H."

"Doing…?"

"Whatever's needed. Dishes. Clearing tables after meals, feeding livestock."

"You sound reluctant."

"I have been, yeah. But lately I'm thinking maybe a job would be a good thing, a way to make sure CJ has a little structure, you know?"

"I think it's a great idea. Teaches him responsibility, gives him a schedule he has to keep. And a little extra pocket change. What's not to like?"

"Well, when you put it that way…" His eyes were soft again. Was that admiration she saw in them? Maybe so, because then he said, "I like the way you dress. In bright colors. Kind of…fun." The way he said *fun* made her absolutely certain that there hadn't been a lot of that in his life.

"I like things bright," she said. "And cheerful."

"And optimistic."

"Yep. That, too." She wondered about his ex-wife,

about what had happened between them that it didn't work out.

But no way was she asking about the ex on a first date. She'd been out with enough men to know the red flags, and a guy talking too much about his ex when a woman hardly knew him was definitely a bad sign. Usually that meant he wasn't over the other woman yet.

He said, "You're looking much too thoughtful."

"Just considering the various conversational booby traps."

"Such as?"

"If I told you, you'd probably only wish I hadn't— and if you *didn't* wish I hadn't, that would be a total red flag."

"I think I'm confused."

"I think I've been on too many first dates."

He laughed. "What? Things never work out for you romantically? I have a hard time believing that."

"Was that compliment?"

"Only the truth as I see it."

She felt absurdly flattered. And her cheeks were warm. And she could sit there forever, looking across the table into Connor McFarlane's sexy, dark eyes, letting the sound of his deep, warm voice pour over her. She said, "It's not that things don't work out for me. It's just, I rarely say no to a first date. So I go on quite a few."

"And second dates?"

"I look at it this way. A first date is one thing. But why say yes to a second when the spark isn't there?"

His gaze remained locked with hers. "I completely agree."

The waiter came and whisked away their plates. He

offered dessert. They both passed, but he had coffee and she took hot tea.

Connor said, "So tell me about Jerilyn. What's her background?"

Something in the way he said that, *What's her background?* had Tori snapping to wary attention. "Jerilyn's a terrific person. Brilliant. Loving. Thoughtful. A straight-A student."

He sipped his coffee. "You sound defensive."

"And you sound like a snob trying to find out if Jerilyn's *background* measures up."

"Tori." His voice was gentle, understanding, even. "She seems like a fine girl."

"She *is* a fine girl."

"And yes, I was wondering about her background."

She poured Earl Grey from the small china teapot into an eggshell-thin cup. "Similar to mine, actually. Her mom died a year ago and her father's having trouble coping."

"What does her father do?"

She looked into his eyes again. And she did not smile. "Butch Doolin is the maintenance engineer at the high school."

"The janitor, you mean."

"It's honest work, Connor."

"Did I say it wasn't?"

Instead of answering him, she sipped her tea. When she gently set the cup back in the saucer, she said, "CJ likes Jerilyn, a lot."

"I noticed."

"And she likes him."

"He's too young for a girlfriend." His voice was gruff.

She argued, "He's old enough to be interested in a girl—in Jerilyn, specifically—which means he's not too young."

"I just don't want him getting into anything serious. Not at his age."

"And especially not with a janitor's daughter." She didn't even try to keep the sarcasm out of her voice.

He sat very still, watching her face. Finally he said, "You're angry."

"Yes. I just saw a side of you I don't like. The elitist side."

"A person's background does matter." His voice was coaxing and kind. She wished she could agree with him, because she really did like him, was seriously attracted to him.

Talk about sparks…

But she couldn't pretend to agree when she didn't. "Background matters up to a point, yes. I wish it didn't, but I'm at least something of a realist. However, what matters most is who that person is. And Jerilyn Doolin is everything I just said she was and more. She's a special girl. It says a lot about your son that he would show the good taste and judgment to have his first big crush on someone like her."

He sat back in his chair and put up both hands. "Okay. I give up. You've convinced me. Jerilyn Doolin is a wonderful girl. CJ is lucky she's interested in him."

Most of her defensive tension drained away. She hid a triumphant smile. "About time you realized that."

"Maybe so." He still looked doubtful.

"But?"

"I'm just not happy about it. CJ can't afford the distraction."

"Distraction? Boys have been falling for girls since the beginning of time. That's not going to change just because you're not happy about it."

"The last thing CJ needs right now is to get too involved with a girl—any girl."

"Connor, he likes her. She likes him. You can't make that go away. In fact, in my experience, which is reasonably extensive given that I work with teenagers for a living, the more the parents try to come between a young couple, the more the attraction grows." Tori spoke with intensity. With passion, even.

He was staring at her, frowning.

Was she becoming a little too emotional over this? Maybe. But she really believed what she was saying and she wanted to get through to the hardheaded man across from her, to get him to understand. She feared if he didn't, he would only be making things worse for CJ.

"*Romeo and Juliet,*" she declared vehemently. "*Wuthering Heights, Titanic.* Think of all the books and plays and movies about passionate, thwarted young love. It only leads to heartbreak when the grown-ups decide to interfere."

He leaned toward her again. "So, Tori."

"What?" she demanded hotly.

"Tell me what you *really* think."

She blinked. And then she laughed. He laughed, too. "Okay," she admitted. "I try to be open-minded, but when I really believe something, I advocate for it, you know?"

"Nothing wrong with that."

She qualified wryly, "Up to a point, you mean."

"Yeah," he agreed. He was watching her mouth again.

"Up to a point…" The words trailed off. A few seconds of silence elapsed—a silence filled with sparks. Finally, he confessed, "Sometimes I'm at a loss, you know? I have no idea how to get through to my own son."

"Are you asking for my advice?"

"Yeah. I guess I am."

"Okay, then. Here's what I think you should do. Take Russ up on his offer to put CJ to work at the Hopping H. And then tell CJ to invite Jerilyn over to your house."

"Over to the house for what?"

"To visit, to hang out. You know, play video games or watch a movie. Make your son feel that his new friends are welcome at home. Let him know that you're on his side. Start changing the equation from you versus him to you supporting him and really taking into account what he wants and needs."

"Seems to me I already support him."

She let her exasperation show. "You mean by buying him every electronic gadget under the sun and then being frustrated because all he does is play video games?"

"What?" Rueful humor shone in his eyes. "I should take away his Xbox?"

"I can't answer that question. You might just widen the rift at this point by denying him something you gave him in the first place."

"Actually, I think that was Jennifer—my ex-wife— who gave him the Xbox."

"Ah. Blaming the ex, huh?"

He shook his head. "Does nothing get by you?"

"Hey, I teach high-school English. Without a sharply honed sense of what's bull and what's not, I wouldn't make it through the first week of a new semester."

He gave in. "Okay, okay. I'll ask CJ to have Jerilyn

over and I'll take Russ up on his offer, get CJ working at Melanie's guest ranch. Anything else?"

Tori laughed. "I'll be in touch with further suggestions."

Entranced. Captivated. Enchanted.

They were words straight out of some women's novel.

But as Connor sat across that table from Tori Jones, he couldn't help thinking that those words exactly described what the small-town schoolteacher did to him. He might as well stop trying to tell himself he wasn't interested. He was powerfully drawn to her.

Clearly, he should have dated more when he was younger.

He'd married Jennifer while they were both in college. Because she was from the right family and she was gorgeous and ready to get married to the right kind of man. A man with money and good breeding equal to her own. It had seemed a very suitable match. The perfect match.

Plus, with the marrying and the settling down out of the way early, he'd been free to concentrate on his career in the family company. He'd never looked at another woman during his marriage. He had a wife and a son, a beautiful home—and his ambitions for McFarlane House, which were considerable. What else was there?

Just possibly, a whole lot more, he was discovering.

There had been a couple of other women, since Jennifer walked out on him. The sex had been good with them, which it never really had been with Jennifer.

But he had never been entranced. Or captivated. Or enchanted.

Until now.

He wanted her—*her,* Tori Jones, in particular. Not just someone suitably attractive and well-bred, as Jennifer had been. Not just someone sophisticated, sexually exciting and discreet, which pretty much described the two women he'd dated after his marriage had crashed and burned.

It came to him that he…he *liked* this woman. And that feeling was new to him. He liked her quick wit, her wisdom and her big heart. He liked the passion in her voice when she talked about things she believed in.

He liked *her.* And suddenly it mattered all out of proportion that she might like him, too.

Was he losing it? He couldn't help but wonder. Was he cracking under the strain—of the soured economy, the McFarlane House setbacks, his divorce, the scary changes in his son? Of the changes he'd decided he needed to make in his life and himself?

Strangely, right then, on his first date with Tori Jones, he didn't care if he just might be going over the edge. He was having a great time—having *fun,* of all things—and he didn't want it to end.

They lingered at the table for over an hour after the meal was finished, talking and laughing, sharing glances that said a lot more than their words did. Finally, reluctantly, he took her home.

At her house, hating to let her go, he walked her up to the door.

She turned to him and said what he'd been praying she might. "Want to come in for a minute?"

He held her gaze, nodded. They shared a warm smile.

Inside, she offered coffee. He accepted, more as a matter of form than because he needed any extra caffeine.

She made more tea for herself and they went out to her comfortable great room and sat on the sofa. He drank the coffee he didn't really want and thought about kissing her, about holding her in his arms.

About how, once he did that, he would have a hard time letting go.

"I should say goodbye," he finally admitted aloud. "It's almost midnight."

"You sure you don't want another cup of coffee?" Those hazel eyes teased him.

"I'm sure." He rose and held down his hand to her. "And it wasn't the coffee I came in for, anyway."

She put her fingers in his. The contact was electric. He had to remind himself forcefully that he was not going to grab her against him and crush her mouth with his. "I'm glad," she said softly as she stood.

He couldn't resist. He lowered his head. She tilted her mouth upward, the sweetest kind of offering.

And, at last, he brushed her lips with his own. Her fresh scent surrounded him and her mouth was soft as rose petals.

She was the one who kept him from deepening that first, too-short kiss. She did that by lowering her head slightly, and taking a step back.

He didn't know whether to applaud her good sense— or reach out and haul her near again. And then she was turning, leading him to the door. He followed.

Out on her front porch, the night was dark velvet.

She touched his arm. The light caress seemed to burn all the way to his soul. "Thank you," she said. "I had a really good time tonight."

"Sunday," he said, his voice lower, rougher than he should have allowed it to be.

"What about it?" She gazed up at him. In her eyes, he saw that if he tried to kiss her again, she would let him.

He didn't try. A little restraint never hurt—or so he told himself. "Melanie's having us out to the Hopping H for a picnic Sunday. CJ and me."

"Great," she said approvingly. "That's what I'm talking about. Make opportunities to spend quality time with him."

"Come with us."

A slight frown tightened her brow and she tipped her head to the side, studying him. "Are you sure? It sounds more like a family thing."

"I'm sure. Come with us. You can keep an eye on me, see how I'm doing, interacting with CJ. Then later, you can give me more advice."

She laughed, the sound like a song in the night. "Oh, so that's it. You want me around to help you improve your relationship with to CJ."

"That's my story and I'm sticking to it. Come with us."

"Why do I get the feeling you're after more than parenting advice from me?"

"Wait."

"For what?"

"For this." He dared to take her gently by the arms and pull her against him. And then he kissed her a second time. A longer kiss. Deeper, too. He wanted to go on like that, kissing her forever in the cool almost-summer darkness. But then he remembered that he was exercising restraint and carefully put her away from him. "I would call that a spark. A definite spark."

"Yeah," she answered breathlessly, her eyes bright as stars. "Guess so."

"So, then. I get a second date, right?"

Her expression turned a little bit sad. "Connor. It's problematic. You know it is."

He told her the straight-ahead truth. "I want to see you again—and not so you can help me out with CJ."

Her eyes widened. But then her soft mouth twisted. "It's only—"

"Say it. Tell me. I can't overcome your objections if you don't tell me what they are."

"Oh, Connor. You're here for the summer and then you'll be gone."

"Just like CJ, with Jerilyn. Why is that okay for them, but not for us?"

"Well, because they're kids and we're not."

"And because we're not kids, we have to live for the future. Is that what you're telling me?"

"No, not exactly. I'm just saying that a summer romance is one thing for two fifteen-year-olds. For adults, it's—"

"What? You won't let yourself live in the moment just because you're all grown up?"

She laughed. "You know, Connor. You can be incredibly persuasive when you put your mind to it."

Triumph flared within him, a sudden bright heat. He was sure he had her. "So that means you'll come with us?"

She glanced out toward the velvety night beyond the

porch, and then met his eyes again. "There's something else."

The flare of triumph died. But he refused to give up. "Tell me."

"I…get a sense that you're a good man deep down. But, well, you're still one of those guys who think they own the world, someone who doesn't care who gets hurt as long as he gets what he wants."

Apparently one of her friends had been saying harsh things about him. Probably whichever friend had told her he was trying to buy out the resort. He wasn't particularly surprised. "Ouch," he said lightly. "Don't feel you have to pull any punches."

"I don't. I won't."

"I noticed." He still wasn't giving up. "You do believe I'm an okay guy—at least, essentially, right?"

"Yes, but—"

"Forget the buts. Just go with that. After all, it's only a second date. Being essentially a good guy should be enough to get me a second date with you—I mean, given the all-important presence of the spark."

"You are incredibly persistent, you know that?"

"I can be, when I want something bad enough."

She moistened her lips. "Um, how bad is bad enough?"

He thought again about another kiss. But he didn't try for one. He only gazed down at her, steadily, trying his best to look both determined and hopeful.

She sighed. "You're right, I suppose."

"Of course I am," he declared with firmness. And then he arched a brow at her. "Er, right about what?"

That soft mouth was trying really hard not to smile.

"Well, that it's only a second date. And there *is* the spark—"

"Exactly. Come with us on Sunday."

She did smile then. For Connor, that smile was like the sun coming out on a rainy day. "Yes," she said. "All right."

Now he had what he wanted, he almost couldn't believe it. He stared down at her, speechless.

"What *are* you thinking?" she demanded, when several seconds had passed without a single word from him.

"You said yes."

"You're surprised?" Her eyes sparkled.

"I guess I am."

"Well, Connor, you were very convincing—but there is a condition."

"Name it."

"I'm inviting Jerilyn, too."

Chapter Four

Connor drove home in a pleasant haze of satisfaction. In spite of her objections, Tori had agreed to a second date. He felt pleased all out of proportion.

And Sunday wouldn't be the end of it. There would be a third date. And a fourth. And more after that. He was certain of it. The summer ahead was looking potentially brighter and more enjoyable than he ever would have imagined.

Until tonight, he'd seen this summer as a series of unpleasant but necessary steps, of things that he needed to do to get his life back on track: to try to get to know his son, to be a better brother to his sister. And to acquire a new property in tough times and make that property profitable in spite of everything.

Now, there was pleasure involved, too. Because of

a certain strawberry-blonde schoolteacher with a cute smattering of freckles across her nose.

At home, Gerda, his live-in housekeeper, was already in bed. Light bled out from under the door of CJ's room. Connor listened for the sounds of weapons firing and objects exploding.

Nothing. Just silence. CJ probably had his headphones on.

He looked at his watch. Almost one.

With a weary sigh, he tapped on the door. No answer. He tapped again, louder.

"What?" Muffled, annoyed, from inside.

Connor pushed the door open and went in.

As expected, CJ sat on the end of the bed, fully dressed, wearing headphones and working a controller. "What?" Eyes on the screen, thumbs flying.

Connor said nothing. He went over and sat next to his son on the bed. He watched the violence on the silent screen while CJ continued to play his game.

Several minutes passed. Connor felt his own impatience rise. He ignored it. He breathed slowly and evenly and he stared at the screen, sitting absolutely still.

Finally, CJ paused the game, took off his headphones, and glared at him. "I asked you, what?"

Connor spoke in a friendly tone. "I had a date with Tori Jones tonight. Had a really good time, too."

CJ gaped. For some reason, Connor found his son's surprise inordinately satisfying. "Ms. Jones? She went out with *you?*"

Connor played it cool. "That's right. And she's coming with us to the picnic Sunday."

"What picnic?" CJ pretended not to remember,

though Connor had told him more than once that they were going.

"Out at the Hopping H."

"Oh, great." Meaning it wasn't. "Forget it, okay? I'm not going to any picnic out at Aunt Melanie's ranch."

"Suit yourself."

CJ slanted him a suspicious look; Connor usually didn't give in that easily.

Connor got up and crossed to the door, turning back to deliver the zinger. "I'm sure Jerilyn will be sorry you couldn't make it." He stepped over the threshold.

CJ stopped him before he shut the door behind him. "Okay, wait."

Connor faced the room again. "It's late. Turn off the game and go to sleep."

"You're serious." CJ squinted at him, as though trying to see inside his head. "Jerilyn will be there."

If she accepts Tori's invitation. "I'm serious."

"Okay, fine. I guess I don't mind going."

Connor remembered Tori's advice. "Another thing."

"What?" CJ asked in a guarded mumble.

"You should ask Jerilyn to come over to the house. And any other new friends you've made in town."

"What for?"

"I don't know, just to…hang out. Plus, I'd like to get to know your friends a little."

CJ frowned as he turned Connor's suggestion over in his mind, no doubt looking for the catch. He found it. "Get to know them? Why? So you can ask them all kinds of questions?"

Connor suppressed a sigh. "No. Because they're your friends, that's all. I would like to meet your friends."

CJ thought about that for a minute. Apparently, he found Connor's reasoning acceptable. He gave out a grudging, "I'll think about it."

"Good. And go to bed."

"Oh, all right." CJ grabbed the remote and turned off the flatscreen.

"Good night," said Connor, as he pulled the door shut after him.

Faintly, he heard his son mutter, "Night."

In the morning, after breakfast, Connor shut the door to his study and called his sister. One of the college girls she had helping out at the ranch for the summer answered the phone.

"Hi, Mr. McFarlane. She's in the dining room, visiting with the guests."

"Have her call me when she gets a moment."

"Hold on. She just came into the kitchen…"

Then Melanie was on the line. "Connor. Hi."

"You sound breathless."

"We've got a full house." Even in the lagging economy, she was making the Hopping H pay. "And it's Saturday breakfast, which is always hectic."

"Just called to give you a heads-up. About tomorrow? I invited two more people. I hope that's okay."

"No problem. The more the merrier. Who? Do I know them?"

"Tori Jones and Jerilyn Doolin."

"Ah," Melanie said. It was a very knowing kind of sound.

"What does *ah* mean?"

"Not a thing."

"Liar."

"Well, if you must know, I ran into Tori at the Tottering Teapot last Monday."

"The Tottering Teapot. Is that a restaurant?"

"That's right. On Main. We all love it."

"We?"

"It's more of a woman's kind of place, actually," she explained. That news didn't surprise him in the least. "Lots of fresh salads. About a thousand different varieties of tea."

"I get the picture," he said without a lot of enthusiasm. "So you talked with Tori…"

"I did. She mentioned she was going out with you. And Grant dropped by early this morning. You two were spotted in the Gallatin Room last night."

He shook his head, though his sister couldn't see. "News travels at the speed of light around this town."

"It does, absolutely." Melanie lowered her voice. "Did you enjoy the evening? Isn't Tori great? I'm glad to see you dating again. It's about time."

"I did. She is. And come on. It's only been a year since the divorce. For your information, I *have* dated before last night, though the two other women I spent time with were nothing like Tori Jones."

"You never told me." She faked a hurt tone.

And suddenly, he could see her as she was at seven or eight years old. A skinny little red-headed thing, wanting attention from her big brother. And never getting it.

He swallowed down the sudden lump of guilt in his throat and kidded her, "Melanie, no matter how well we get along now, I'm not telling you everything."

"And just when I thought I knew all your secrets." Her joking tone turned distracted. "Hold on a minute…"

He heard her giving instructions to someone. Then she came back on the line. "Where were we?"

"I'm not going to keep you. But I did want to ask…"

"What? Name it."

"About that job offer Russ made, for CJ?"

"Still open. Just say the word."

"Great. But I'm thinking CJ's more likely to agree to the idea if it comes straight from you—or from anyone but me. Somehow, whatever I say to him nowadays, he thinks it's an order. An order he's honor-bound to reject out of hand."

"All right, then. Sunday, when the time is right, I'll offer him a job."

Tori called Jerilyn at nine Saturday morning to invite her to the Sunday picnic at Melanie's guest ranch.

The teenager answered the phone in tears. "Oh, Ms. Jones, I don't know what to do…"

"What? What's the matter?"

"Can I…would it be all right if I came over?"

"Yes. Right now. Do you want me to come and get you?"

"Oh, no. It's okay." The girl paused to stifle a sob. "I can ride my bike. I'll be there in ten minutes."

"You're sure?"

"I'll be right over."

When Jerilyn appeared, pedaling fast down the street, Tori was waiting for her, out on the porch.

"Oh, Ms. Jones…" Jerilyn dropped her bike on the front walk. Fresh tears welled. She ran up the steps and into Tori's waiting arms.

Tori pulled the girl inside and shut the door. "Shh… shh. There now. Okay…"

When the sobbing settled down a little, Tori led her to the sofa, passed the tissues, and got the story out of her.

"My dad got a warning Thursday. From his supervisor. My dad hasn't been getting the summer maintenance done. And if his work doesn't improve in the next two weeks, he's going to get fired."

"Oh, Jerilyn." Tori hugged her again. "Did your dad tell you this?"

Jerilyn blew her nose. "No way. He doesn't tell me anything. I found the warning notice on the kitchen table, wadded up in a ball. And he started drinking Thursday night. He called in sick yesterday. He drank all day, late into last night. He was still at it when I finally went to bed. This morning, he won't get up. I made breakfast. Just what he likes, scrambled eggs and home fries, sausage and English muffins. I tried to get him up to eat. He just growled at me to leave him alone."

"Has he…hit you?" Tori hated to ask, but she knew that she had to. "Or hurt you in any way?"

Jerilyn sobbed and shook her head. "Oh, no. He just sits at the kitchen table and drinks and doesn't say anything. Sometimes…he cries."

Tori grabbed her close again. "Aw, honey. It's okay. It's okay." As she gave out the familiar litany of reassurances, she knew that in reality, it wasn't okay. Not okay in the least.

"He would never hurt me." Jerilyn swallowed more sobs. "Except that when he loses his job and we can't pay the bills and…well, that will hurt me. That will hurt me really bad."

"That's not going to happen."

Jerilyn sagged against Tori with a long, sad sigh. "Yeah. It is. It is going to happen."

Tori took her by the shoulders. "Look at me. Do you trust me?"

"You know I do. Totally."

"I'm going to call someone who can help, okay? I'm going to do everything I can to bring your dad back to you, to make sure he doesn't lose his job."

Jerilyn blinked away the tears. "Who are you going to call?"

"Someone who's been through exactly what your dad's going through. Someone who managed to survive. Someone who will know what to do."

Tori's father, Dr. Sherwood Jones, caught a one-o'clock flight to Bozeman and rented a car. By four that afternoon, he was sitting in Tori's living room.

"I can't promise anything," he warned a pale-faced Jerilyn, who looked at him through red, puffy eyes. "And I can't even talk to him unless he's sober."

"He should be, by now. Unless he's started in drinking again."

"You say he's never hit you or been in any way violent with you?"

"No. He wouldn't. He…hasn't. Not ever. He's just so sad and lonely for my mom. They were always so close. She was his very best friend in the world. Without her… it's killing him, Dr. Jones. It's hurting him so deep."

"I understand." He glanced over at Tori, who sat across the coffee table from him and Jerilyn. Tori gulped down the sudden lump in her throat. Her dad did understand. They both did. He told Jerilyn. "Tori and I lost her mother when Tori was a couple of years younger than you are."

Jerilyn's eyes filled with tears again. She turned her gaze to Tori and tried a wobbly smile. "I know. Ms. Jones told me that, right after my mom died."

Sherwood clasped Jerilyn's shoulder. "I think we should go to your house now, see if maybe your dad is sober, and willing to talk with me. Are you okay with doing that?"

Jerilyn's dark eyes were wide—and determined. "Yes. I think we should. We should go now."

"Well, all right then," Sherwood said, with that gentle smile that always warmed Tori's heart.

They were at the front door when the phone rang. Tori told them, "I'll just get that and be out in a sec."

Her dad and Jerilyn headed for the car as Tori answered the phone on the side table in the great room.

It was Connor. "I just called to tell you I really hope Jerilyn said yes about tomorrow. I told CJ she would be there and suddenly he can't wait to go to a picnic at the Hopping H."

His voice, so warm, threaded with wry humor, made her wish he was there, right then, at her side. She would lean into him and he would put his strong arms around her and she would feel she could handle anything, even the rough family problems of her star student—and what was she thinking?

He was never going to be the kind of man she could lean on. She really had to remember that. He was leaving when summer was over—and in the meantime, he was going to cause trouble in the town that she loved.

"Tori? You there?"

"Right here. I…haven't invited her yet."

"What is it? What's happened?"

"It's a long story, one I just don't have time to go into right now."

"What can I do? Anything."

She almost smiled. When he talked like that, so ready to rush to her side if she needed him, she could almost forget that in his real life, he was a ruthless corporate shark determined to buy out the Thunder Canyon Resort and throw a bunch of people out of work. "No, really. Thank you."

"Are you in trouble?"

"No. Don't worry, please. It's not about me. I'm perfectly okay. And I'll explain it all later. Right now, I have to go."

"Call me. As soon as you can. I mean it."

"Yes. All right. I'll call this evening. I promise." She said a hurried goodbye and then rushed out to join and Jerilyn and Sherwood in his rental car.

Jerilyn lived in a small, run-down house in a South New Town neighborhood that had seen better days. The siding needed fresh paint and the porch boards creaked.

Inside, they found Butch Doolin sitting at the cluttered kitchen table in a T-shirt and a ragged pair of sweatpants. His bloodshot eyes were puffy from too much alcohol the day before and he sported a couple of days' worth of dark beard.

But he had a cup of coffee in front of him—no liquor in sight. He looked hungover, but sober.

And more than a little surprised to see Jerilyn, her teacher and some man he'd never met before standing in the doorway to his living room. "Jerilyn? What's going on?"

Tori's dad stepped right up. "I'm Sherwood Jones, Mr. Doolin. We're here to see if we can help."

Butch frowned. "Help?" And then he slowly shook his head. He turned to Jerilyn and spoke with weary resignation. "Sweet girl, what have you been up to?"

Jerilyn put her hand over her mouth, swallowed hard, and then let her hand drop. "Daddy. I saw that warning letter. You're going to lose your job. I had to do something. You can't keep on like this."

Tori had never seen a man so shamed as Butch Doolin was right then. He hung his head. "Sweet girl, I'm so sorry. So damn sorry. I don't know what to do, how to keep going. Without your mother, it all seems so pointless…" His big shoulders shook.

Jerilyn would have gone to him. But Tori's dad stopped her. He tipped his head back the way they had come. "You two go ahead," he said low. "Let me talk to him for a while." He tossed Tori the keys to the rental car. "I'll call you…"

Tori took Jerilyn's hand and led her back out through the small, dim living room. They returned to Tori's house to wait. Time crawled by. Tori offered dinner, but Jerilyn only shook her head.

Finally, at a little after seven, Tori's dad called for them to come and get him. Sherwood Jones was waiting for them out in front when they got to Jerilyn's again.

Jerilyn jumped out. "My dad? Is he…?"

Tori got out, too, and came around to join them on the cracked sidewalk.

"Your dad is okay. And I think he's going to be a lot better, Jerilyn," Tori's dad said. "I think he's ready to get help. We talked for a long time. He poured out all the booze in the house and he'll be going to regular AA meetings. Plus I've given him the names of a few good counselors he can choose from, as well as a local grief recovery group. And he has my number. I'm always available to him if he needs me." He gave Jerilyn a card. "And I'm available for you, as well. You can call me here, directly, if there's anything you want to ask me. And especially if you find yourself worried about him again."

"You really think he's going to get better?"

"I do. Sincerely. It's not going to be easy, but I think you'll see a definite improvement now."

Jerilyn let out a low cry and grabbed Tori's father in a hug. "Thank you, oh, thank you."

He hugged her back. "Call me if you need help. I mean that."

Then Tori offered Jerilyn that dinner she hadn't accepted before, but she was eager to go in, to talk to her dad. She grabbed Tori close, quickly let her go and turned for the house.

Tori remembered the picnic tomorrow. "Wait. I almost forgot. You're invited to a picnic at the Hopping H tomorrow."

"Will CJ be there?" The sad dark eyes were suddenly brighter.

"Yeah. But I'm sure he'll understand, if you'd rather—"

Jerilyn put up a hand. "Please. I want to go. My bike's at your house. Can you pick me up?"

Tori named a time and Jerilyn said she would be ready.

As Tori and her dad got back in the rental, she offered, "Hungry?"

Her dad shook his head. "Butch gave me a sandwich. And I need to get to Bozeman. There's a flight to Denver at ten to nine."

They drove back to Tori's house.

"That's one shiny SUV," her dad said when he pulled to a stop behind the expensive vehicle. "And there's a man on your porch."

Tori glanced over and saw Connor sitting on her top step, wearing pricey jeans, expensive boots and a dark-colored knit shirt. The sight of him caused her heart to do a happy somersault inside her chest. Which was ridiculous. *And* physically impossible. "It's Connor. He's…a friend," she said, sounding absurdly breathless. Connor rose and came down the steps. She added, "I'll introduce you to him, Dad."

Connor was already at her side door. She rolled her window down. He was smiling. But his eyes were cool. Maybe he wasn't all that happy about watching her drive up with a strange man.

"Hey," he said. "I got worried about you."

"Connor, this is my father, Dr. Sherwood Jones."

Suddenly, his dark eyes had warmth in them again. "Dr. Jones. Hello."

Her dad stuck his arm across the seat. "Good to meet you, Connor." Connor put out his hand, too. Tori leaned out of the way so they could shake.

Then Sherwood gunned the engine. "I hate to run off. But I have to get a move on or I'll miss that last flight. And while your stepmother is a very understanding woman, she insists I save Sundays for her and the boys."

Tori leaned across the console and kissed his cheek. "Thanks, Dad."

"Anytime."

"Kiss Lucille and hug my brothers for me."

"Will do."

Connor opened her door for her and she got out. With a final wave, Tori's dad drove off.

She felt Connor's hand settle at her waist. A little thrill went through her at the contact. She chided him, "I said I would call."

"I should be more patient, I know."

"Yes, you should. Especially considering that we've only had one date."

"Two, if you count tomorrow."

She laughed. "It's not tomorrow yet." And then she confessed, "I'm glad you're here."

"Me, too." He pulled her closer to his side. "What was that all about?"

She looked up into those beautiful eyes of his and wanted to trust him—even if he *was* a shark. "I'm starving."

"Are you going to tell me what happened today?"

"Probably. But right now, I want to eat."

"You want to go out?"

"You know, you're sneaking in a third date on me and we haven't even gotten through the second one yet."

"It's true. That's exactly what I'm doing. We could go to—"

She didn't let him finish. "No. I've got some stuffed shells in the fridge. And I'll make a salad. You want pasta?"

"I ate with CJ. But if you twisted my arm, I'd have a little something."

"Jerilyn will be coming with us tomorrow."

"Terrific. I wasn't looking forward to telling CJ otherwise."

They went up the walk together, circling Jerilyn's bike when they got to it. Tori made a mental note to take it up to the porch before she went to bed.

Inside, Connor pushed the front door shut behind them and caught her hand when she would have headed straight for the kitchen.

"Wait a minute…" His warm, strong arms came around her.

"Oh, Connor…"

"Shh." He lowered his mouth to hers.

It was a beautiful kiss. Slow, lazy, gradually deepening. His arms felt so good around her and her body seemed to hum in response to him, as if she were somehow tuned to him—to his touch, to his strong body pressed so close to hers, to his lips that were doing magical things to hers. Even to the scent of him, which was clean and so manly. He tasted of mint. And of heat. She never wanted to pull away.

But she did. "Dinner. I mean it."

In the kitchen, she warmed up the giant herb-and-cheese stuffed pasta shells and put a salad together. He ate two shells and two pieces of garlic bread. She sat across from him at her breakfast nook table and couldn't believe how comfortable it felt having him there.

Comfortable. And kind of thrilling. Both at the same time.

Was that good?

Or just plain dangerous? The last thing she needed was to fall for Connor McFarlane, who would wreak havoc up at the resort, cause people to lose their livelihoods—and then go back east before the first snow.

"Does Melanie know you're planning to take over the resort?"

He set down his fork. "The shells were really good. And who says I'm planning to take over the resort?"

"Well, if you were—and she didn't know—that might not be such a great thing for your relationship with her, that you might be doing something that affects her community and you haven't even bothered to tell her. I mean, if you're not going tell me, you at least should tell *her* what you're up to, don't you think?"

He had picked up his water glass. But he set it down without taking a drink. "Yes," he said blandly. "I suppose, if I were planning a buyout of the resort, that maybe I ought to tell my sister what I have in mind."

"Will you, then? Will you tell her?"

He only gazed at her, his face a mask, unreadable.

Suddenly, she was furious with him. But why?

Self-preservation, maybe. She could still feel the warm, exciting pressure of his lips on hers, still remember the thrill of his arms wrapped tightly around her.

Really, she was much too attracted for her own peace of mind.

She said, too softly, "You want me to tell you what happened this afternoon, to trust you with something that's private to someone I care about, but you won't even tell me honestly whether you're thinking of buying out the resort or not."

He took his napkin from his lap, wiped his mouth, and slid it in beside his plate. "All right, Tori."

"All right, what?"

"I can see this is an ultimatum."

"I didn't say that."

"You didn't have to. It's all over your face, clear in your voice."

"Look. The word is out that you're sniffing around the resort. People aren't blind around here. And if I'm going to be spending more time with you, I want to know the truth. I can live with this thing between us ending when the fall comes. But I can't live with you lying to me."

"I haven't lied to you."

"By omission, yes. You have. I want to know for certain. I *need* to know—at least, I do if we're going to keep dating."

"Why do you need to know? What possible good will the information do?"

She considered his question. And she answered truthfully. "It's about honesty, Connor. It's about basic trust. Are you hoping to buy out the resort, yes or no?"

A silence. A long one. And then, finally, "I would need to know ahead of time that you would keep what I tell you to yourself."

"Uh-uh. No way. Is there some reason it has to be a secret—especially considering that everybody already knows anyway? I mean, come on. You talk about how you want to change things in your life, with your son. With your sister. Maybe being straight in your business dealings wouldn't be such a bad idea, either. I'm not saying you have to tell me all the diabolical details of your takeover plan. I'm just saying why deny what you're after when everyone knows your denial is a big, fat lie anyway?"

He arched a brow. "Diabolical?"

She waved a hand. "Sorry. That was a little over the top. But still, you know what I mean."

He refused to give in. "As a rule, it's not a good idea to show your hand, even if the player across from you already knows you have aces."

"We're talking about people's lives, Connor, not a card game."

He pushed back his chair and stood. "This conversation is going nowhere."

She knew he was right. They were arguing in circles. She said gently, "Yeah. I guess so."

"Good night." His voice was soft, his eyes troubled.

"Good night, Connor."

He went out through the great room. She heard the front door open and close. And a minute or two after that, she heard the SUV start up and drive away.

She sat there at the table for a long time after he left her, feeling sad and weepy—but refusing to cry. Connor McFarlane was not the man for her. She had to accept that. It was better that he had left, that his thing between them went no further. Getting into it with him would only lead to hurt and heartbreak.

Alone at the table, she nodded to herself and swallowed down the lump of tears that clogged her throat. Yes. Really. It was better that he was gone.

Chapter Five

Connor was halfway back to his rented house, feeling like crap, trying to come to grips with the fact that his enjoyable summer with Tori Jones was over before it had even begun, when he realized that he'd left her without canceling their plans for tomorrow.

At the house, after spending a few minutes in CJ's room, watching him play his endless video game, he went to his own room. He took a shower and sat in front of the television, channel-surfing with the sound down, paying very little attention to the images that flashed in front of his eyes.

He kept reliving what it felt like to hold her in his arms. He'd been really looking forward to doing that again, and frequently. And he'd done some serious fantasizing over what it was going to be like the first time they made love. It would probably be really good, if the chemistry between them was any indication.

Maybe she would call and tell him formally that she wouldn't be coming to the picnic tomorrow. Maybe he ought to call her.

But the phone didn't ring. And he decided it would be easier just to go ahead and proceed as planned tomorrow. At worst, she would call it off when he and CJ came to pick her and Jerilyn up. He could live with that.

And if she decided to go through with it, well, he could stand that, too. It would be awkward, yes, but at least CJ would be happy to have some time with the girl he liked.

In the morning, Connor had breakfast with CJ and then went to his study to look over some paperwork from the main office. The phone rang at eleven. He jumped at the sound.

But it was only his father, making the usual demands, that he come back to Philly immediately, to stay. That, if he insisted on doing the resort deal, he get on it and get it over with.

Connor made noncommittal noises and told his dad to give his mother his love.

An hour later, he and CJ left the house.

"You okay, Dad?" CJ asked him as they drove the quiet Sunday streets on the way to Tori's house.

Connor almost ran a red light. It was the first time in the past year or so that his son had expressed the slightest interest in him or anything he might be doing or thinking.

It was a clear sign that he was actually making progress with the boy. He should have been ecstatic.

And he was. But the thrill was muted by the

knowledge that whatever progress he was making with CJ was mostly due to the excellent advice of a certain strawberry-blonde schoolteacher. And then there was also the possibility that whatever gains he'd made would be lost if Jerilyn was not at Tori's house when they got there, if Tori had decided to call the afternoon off.

Really, he should have discussed the picnic with her before he walked out on her last night. Or called her later.

But he hadn't. And now he was stuck with having no clue what would happen when they got to her house.

Bright move, McFarlane.

He pushed his dark thoughts away and sent his son a warm glance. "Thanks, I'm okay."

"You're really quiet."

"Just…thoughtful, I guess."

At Tori's house, the bicycle that had been on the front walk the evening before was propped up on the porch. But other than that, everything looked just as it had last night. He still had no clue whether Tori and Jerilyn were coming with them, or not.

CJ jumped out of the car and was halfway up the walk before Connor got out and followed him. It was CJ who rang the doorbell. Connor was just climbing the steps when the door opened.

Tori, in jeans, boots and a cute, snug Western shirt, grinned at CJ. "Right on time."

Relief, sweet as cool water on a hot day, poured through Connor. They were going. He'd never been so pleased about anything in his life.

Jerilyn, also in jeans, peered over Tori's shoulder. "Hey."

"Hey," CJ replied, his voice cracking on the

single syllable. He cleared his throat and said it again. "Hey."

Tori's gaze shifted to meet Connor's. She gave him a careful smile and a nod. He did the same.

"I packed a basket," she said. "Some cheese and fruit, some whole-wheat crackers. Some juice…"

Jerilyn pulled a face. "All totally healthy," she added. And she and CJ groaned in unison.

"Ready to go?" Connor asked.

"Yes, we are," Tori replied, her gaze sliding away from his. "I'll get the basket and we can be on our way."

His relief that she wasn't backing out on him faded. He could see the day stretching endlessly out ahead of them. A day of careful smiles and sliding glances, of unacknowledged tension.

But there was nothing else to do but gut it up and get through it. The muscles in his shoulders knotting, he turned and went back down the steps toward the waiting SUV.

It was a good day, the sky clear and blue, with only a few fluffy white clouds gliding slowly toward the west.

Russ had horses picked out and tacked up for each of them. Connor, who had learned to ride six years before when he opened McFarlane House Louisville at a former horse ranch, got a big palomino mare. Tori got a handsome bay gelding. CJ's gray seemed calm and steady-natured, as did Jerilyn's blue roan. Russ, Melanie and Ryan all rode the horses they favored for everyday riding at the Hopping H and at Russ's original ranch, the Flying J, which abutted the H.

Melanie had pack saddles full of food and drinks. She tucked the stuff Tori had brought in with the rest, and they rode out.

In a wide, rolling pasture dotted with wildflowers, they spread a couple of blankets. Melanie and Tori put out the food. They ate as the hobbled horses cropped the grass nearby.

The kids were finished with lunch in no time. They wandered off to explore, CJ and Jerilyn side by side, Ryan happily trailing along behind.

The grown-ups chatted about casual stuff. Melanie said she and Russ were turning a nice profit with the guest ranch. Russ talked about buying more land. Connor dared to kid him that if he didn't watch out, he'd become a land baron. Russ laughed and said maybe he would. His easy response pleased Connor. He was making progress healing the early breach with his cowboy brother-in-law.

Tori mentioned some Outward Bound–type program, ROOTS, that a local woman, Haley Anderson, was trying to start up in a storefront in town. Melanie said she was so happy for Haley, to have found the right place for ROOTS at last.

And then Melanie wanted to know if Tori had met Erin Castro, who was new in town and apparently going around asking questions about the Cateses, the Cliftons and the Traubs.

Tori frowned. "No. I haven't met her."

Russ said, "Grant told me that woman started in on him at the Hitching Post. She had a thousand and one questions."

Connor remembered the blonde woman he'd spoken to at the bar at DJ's. "I met her at the summer kickoff barbecue. She introduced herself." He described their brief conversation.

Russ grunted. "She's up to something..."

"But what?" Melanie wondered aloud.

Russ added, "Grant said she has this tattered yellowed newspaper clipping, a picture of some old-time gathering of—"

"Let me guess." Connor predicted, "The Cateses, the Cliftons and the Traubs."

"You got it."

"Maybe she's writing a tell-all," Tori suggested lightly. "The secrets of Thunder Canyon, Montana, revealed."

"She better watch herself," Russ muttered darkly. "Folks around here don't like strangers poking in their private business."

And the conversation moved on.

Connor didn't say much to Tori. She returned the favor. He didn't think his sister or her husband even noticed that they kept their distance from each other and avoided eye contact.

He couldn't help glancing Tori's way, though, when he thought no one was looking. She was so pretty, strawberry-blond hair shining in the sun, her skin like cream. There was something about her, even beyond her fresh good looks, something that drew him. He couldn't explain it, and he certainly didn't understand it. It just *was,* like the blue sky above, the wide, rolling pasture below.

And it's going nowhere, so get over it, the voice of wisdom within advised.

The kids wandered in and out of their view, sometimes disappearing into a small stand of pines on a ridge to the northeast, sometimes coming near, but then turning to head off in a different direction before they got too close to the adults. Their laughter and chatter rang out across the rolling field.

Once, when they were all three in sight, near a weathered fence that separated the pasture from the next one over, Melanie got up. "Time to talk a little business." She set off toward the three by the fence.

"Business?" Tori glanced at Connor—and then apparently caught herself actually looking at him. Her gaze slid away.

Russ, stretched out on his back, with his hat over his eyes, said lazily, "Connor's decided it's not a bad idea if CJ does a little honest work this summer."

Tori sent Connor another swift glance. What? She was surprised that he'd taken her advice.

He gave a curt nod and looked away.

Russ, still with his hat over his eyes, continued, "He and Red agreed that she should make the offer." According to Melanie, Russ had always called her Red. Even back when she didn't like it in the least. Now, though, it was his pet name for her.

Melanie had reached the three teenagers. Connor— and Tori, too, he noticed out of the corner of his eye— watched as the scene played out. Melanie spoke.

CJ instantly started shaking his head, backing away. It looked like a no-go.

But then Jerilyn said something. Melanie nodded and offered her hand. The girl took it.

And then CJ spoke up again. Melanie turned to him and said something. He nodded. And Melanie shook *his* hand.

Ryan shot a fist in the air and they heard him exclaim, "Yes!"

Russ lifted his hat enough to glance toward the scene by the old fence. "Mission accomplished, if you ask me."

"Looks that way," Connor agreed. "Your wife is amazing."

"She certainly is." Russ spoke with deep satisfaction. Then he put his hat back over his eyes and let his head drop to the blanket again.

Melanie returned to them. Connor thought she looked sort of bemused. "CJ starts tomorrow," she told him. "Nine to one, Monday through Thursday. I guess we'll have to take turns driving him out here—Jerilyn, too."

"Either Gerda or I will do it, no problem." Connor would slip his housekeeper a little extra for the inconvenience. "So you've got two new employees, then?"

"Oh, yes, I do. CJ turned me down flat. But then Jerilyn spoke up and said how she'd love to work at the Hopping H. So I offered her the job."

Connor could guess the rest. "And then CJ suddenly changed his mind."

"And it's great. I can put them both to work, and Ryan will love having them around." She added, sounding bemused again, "I really do like that girl."

Connor almost turned to share a glance with Tori, to give her a nod of acknowledgment, since what had just happened was all at her urging. But then he remembered that he and Tori were finished sharing glances.

They were finished, period.

As the day went by, Tori became only more certain that there really was no hope for her and Connor. The picnic at the ranch was just one of those final obligations they both felt duty-bound to fulfill.

By Sunday evening, when Connor pulled the SUV to a stop in front of her house, she was beyond positive. It was done between them, finished. All without ever really getting started.

She tried to remind herself yet again that it was for the best. But somehow it didn't feel that way in the least.

CJ and Jerilyn jumped out first, but only to load Jerilyn's bike in the back. They would take it to her house when they dropped her off.

That left Tori and Connor momentarily alone.

She said, each word falsely bright, "Well, thank you. It was a beautiful day."

"Yeah," he replied without looking at her. "Great weather."

"I'll be seeing you, then." She leaned on the door.

He turned as the door swung wide and he looked at her. A look that burned her right down to the core. She had the impossible, overwhelming urge to leap across the console and kiss him so hard...

Uh-uh. No way. Not going to happen.

She tore her gaze free of his and got the heck out of there, somehow managing to wave goodbye to Jerilyn and CJ as they put the bike in the back of the SUV.

In the house, feeling totally bereft and hating that she felt that way, she called Allaire. But no one was home. They were probably off at some Traub family Sunday dinner. Tori hung up without leaving a message.

About then, she realized that she'd left her picnic basket in the back of Connor's SUV. It wasn't a big deal. She could get it later. Much, much later.

Or maybe he would have CJ drop it by.

It was all just too sad and depressing. She'd finally found a guy who made her heart turn somersaults, and he was a ruthless corporate shark unwilling to be straight with her.

She took a long bath and turned in early.

And at midnight she was still lying there, wide awake, telling herself that she hardly knew Connor. They'd only spent a total of maybe fifteen hours together—if you counted the picnic just that day, when they'd each been doing their level best to pretend the other didn't exist.

Really, she needed to get over this and move on. She needed to shut her eyes and get some sleep.

But sleep was not in the offing. She kept seeing his face at that last moment before she got out of the SUV, seeing the hunger there, the stark longing for what was never going to happen between them. She kept thinking that maybe she had been too uncompromising.

After all, she knew darn well he was trying to buy out the resort. His confessing the fact in so many words wouldn't make much difference in the end.

Except that, well, what kind of relationship would they have, if he couldn't even be honest with her about his real intentions? It all had to start with honesty, and with trust, too. If they didn't have honesty and trust, they had nothing.

Time crawled by. She tried not to look at her bedside clock. It only reminded her how miserable she was—and how little sleep she was getting.

And then, out of nowhere, at ten after one, the door-bell rang.

At the unexpected sound, her pulse started booming in her ears. And her chest felt so tight, it hurt to breathe.

Either it was Connor, unable to wait to tell her he wanted to work it out with her. Or it was some awful disaster that couldn't be put off till daylight: a fire; Jerilyn with bad news about her dad...

Terrible dread and impossible hope warring for prominence in her heart, Tori yanked on her robe and ran to answer. Breathless, frantic, she pulled the door wide—and when she saw who was on the other side, her pulse thudded all the louder.

Connor.

He stood there on her doorstep in the same jeans and fancy boots he'd worn that afternoon, her picnic basket in his hand, looking exhausted—but determined, too. She realized as she gaped at him that he was the handsomest man she'd ever known.

"You left this in my SUV." He held out the basket. "And yes, I'm planning to buy the resort."

Connor waited, his stomach in a knot and his throat locked up tight. He had no idea what would happen next. She just might grab the basket and shut the door in his face.

But no. Those amazing hazel eyes had gone misty. That had to be a good sign, right?

And then she stepped back and tipped her head toward the great room, inviting him in.

He cleared his throat. He felt he owed her...something. A more thorough confession.

What the hell was happening to him? He wished he knew.

He found his voice. "I've been walking the floor half the night, thinking about you—" And then it was like a damn bursting. The words came tumbling out of him.

"Thinking about how I've never met anyone like you and I can't stand to think it's over with us when it never even got started. I decided at least fifty times that I would come over here—after which I decided not to, that in the end, I would be leaving when the summer is over, so what was the point, since I know you want more than a summer romance?"

She gazed up at him, her eyes so soft. "Connor."

"Yeah?"

"Will you please come in so that I can shut the door?"

He frowned, wanting—*needing*—her to be certain about letting him into her house. It was insane. Where had these silly scruples come from? He'd never been troubled by them before. "You're, uh, sure?"

She only looked at him, still misty-eyed, and slowly nodded her red-gold head.

So he stepped over the threshold. She shut the door behind him and turned the lock. And then she took the picnic basket from him and set it on the narrow entry-area table.

"Come on." She turned. He followed her through the great room to her cozy kitchen at the back of the house. "Sit down." She gestured at the table.

He sat, hardly daring to believe he was actually here in her kitchen again, that not only had he come here in the middle of the night, she had answered the door. She had let him in.

Maybe it wasn't over, after all.

He watched, dumbfounded, as she put water on for the tea she liked and loaded up the coffeemaker for him. She looked more beautiful than ever, he thought, with her hair a little wild, her face scrubbed clean of makeup, wearing a lightweight yellow robe that revealed a lot of sleek bare leg and adorable bare feet with toenails painted the color of a ripe plum.

She pushed the brew button on the coffeemaker and took the chair across from him. "What else?"

"Uh. Excuse me?"

"It seemed as though you had more to say."

"I did. I do."

She folded her hands on the tabletop. "I'm listening."

He raked his fingers back through his hair. "It's only…I'm sorry, but I can't give you more than this summer. This, right now, that's all I'm ready for. I'm not…cut out for anything more."

Her red-kissed brows drew together and he knew he wasn't making much sense.

He confessed, "I, well, I was a lousy husband, you know?"

"No. I didn't know."

"I was. Just lousy. All that really mattered to me was my work. I wanted to take what my father and grandfather had started and make it *more*. New, exciting locations, each one-of-a-kind, each a luxury boutique hotel with stylish rooms, signature restaurants, bars and destination spas. I considered marriage and children as no more than something that was expected of me, something I needed to get out of the way so I could focus on my work, on growing the McFarlane House brand. So I fulfilled what I saw as my obligation to acquire a spouse, to procreate. I found a beautiful woman with the right pedigree and I married her."

"You…you didn't care for her at all?"

He shrugged. "Looking back, I think I told myself I

cared. But really, being brutally honest now, I didn't care enough. Yes, I told my ex-wife I loved her, but it was just because I knew it was something I was supposed to say. And it's only by necessity that I'm trying to figure out how to be a halfway decent dad for CJ."

"But, Connor, you *are* trying. That's what matters."

"No. I'm doing what I have to do, fulfilling my responsibility to my son. Period. I live for my work, and I'm not husband material. I can't see that changing. I'm just not a family man."

She caught her lower lip between her even white teeth—and then let it go. "Clearly, it's not going to do any good to tell you that you're a better man than you think you are."

He stuck with the truth, painful as it was to reveal. "I think you *want* me to be a better man."

She gazed at him for a long time. And then, finally, she conceded, "Yes. That may be true, to an extent. I would like you to be the best you can be. Tonight, though, I see that you already are a good man. A man capable of honesty. Of trust. And I understand what you're telling me. I already knew—or at least, I knew the part about how you're not up for anything long-lasting. We talked about it before, remember?"

"Of course I remember. I remember everything. Every look. Every smile. Every word we said." He swore low. "I sound like an idiot, some hopeless fool…"

"No. You don't." She reached out her hand to him. He met her halfway, in the middle of the table. Palm to palm, they wove their fingers together. "You don't sound like a fool, not in the least." Her soft mouth trembled on a smile. "I'm so glad that you're here. That it's not over, after all."

He shoved back his chair and stood. She stood with him. And then, hands still joined, in unison they stepped toward each other around the table. Once she was close enough, he reeled her in. She felt like heaven in his arms.

"No, it's not over," he said, staring down into those beautiful misty eyes. "Not yet…"

"Not yet…" she echoed, lifting her mouth to him. He took it. Wrapping her tighter, closer, he kissed her deeply, learning all the sweet, wet surfaces behind her parted lips.

When he lifted his head, it was only to slant it the other way and claim her lips again. He could have stood there in her kitchen, holding her, kissing her, until the sun came up.

But then the kettle whistled and the coffeemaker beeped. He let her go so she could brew her tea and pour his coffee.

They sat across from each other again.

He stared at his untouched mug, at the fragrant curl of steam rising from it. "Jerilyn told CJ what happened Saturday, the crisis with Jerilyn's father. He said your dad flew in from Denver to help. Jerilyn says she has hope now, that things will be all right."

"CJ told you what Jerilyn told him?"

"He did."

"I think I would call that actual communication—and the beginnings of trust, as well."

"So would I. Due in large part to you, Tori. I'm trying, I really am, to take your advice, to let him know I'm on his side, that he can count on me. I think it just may be working—at least a little."

"I'm so glad."

"You haven't touched your tea."

She tipped her head to the side the way she always did when she was studying him. "And you aren't drinking your coffee."

He confessed, "I'm thinking about holding you in my arms again. And I'm also thinking that if I start kissing you, I won't want to stop."

"Would that be…so bad?" Her voice was shy, hesitant. Her eyes were anything but.

"Uh-uh. Not bad at all. It would be really, really good. But I don't want to rush you into anything you might regret."

Her smile was full of feminine intent. "How long do you plan to stay here in town?"

"I have to leave Wednesday, for meetings in Philadelphia. But I'll be back by Friday afternoon."

Steadily, she held his gaze. "I meant, how long are you planning to be living in town? When will you be leaving for good?"

"If the resort deal works out, I'll be here into the winter, at least. But after CJ returns to school, I'll make my home base back east, and only be in Thunder Canyon on and off."

"And CJ starts school…?"

"At the end of August."

"A little over two months from now."

"That's right. Is that somehow significant?"

"Yes. Very."

"Because?"

She pushed her chair back again, leaving her tea still untouched. "Because two months will go by too fast. And it seems to me that we shouldn't waste a day, an hour, another *minute* of the time we have together."

He stared at her. And then, slowly, he rose to his feet. They faced each other, with only the round kitchen table between them. He asked, rough and low, "What are telling me, Tori?"

She approached him slowly, untying the sash of her robe as she came. When she reached him, she dropped the sash to the floor and eased the robe from her shoulders. It fell away without a sound. Underneath she wore a short summer nightgown with tiny satin straps that tied in charming little bows at her shoulders. That nightgown revealed a lot more than it covered.

His desire, carefully banked until then, flared high. "You are so beautiful."

"Take me in your arms, Connor," she whispered, lifting on tiptoe, her breasts brushing his chest, making the flare of desire burn all the hotter. "Take me in your arms and hold me all night long."

Chapter Six

Connor's newfound conscience urged him to argue with her, to tell her she ought to think twice about this, to grab her by the shoulders and put her firmly away from him, to speak reasonably about taking their time, to remind her again about not rushing into anything she might regret later.

But she had it right, after all. They didn't have a lot of time. Just one short summer.

And wasting a minute of it, now they were both on the same page about where they were going?

Uh-uh. No way.

He wrapped his arms around her, good and tight. And he kissed her, deeply. Endlessly. His mouth locked to hers, drinking her in, he bent to scoop her up high in his arms.

She pulled her soft lips from his just long enough

to fling out a hand in the general direction of the great room and to whisper, "That way…"

He claimed her mouth again and started walking, carrying her out of the kitchen, across the great room, to her bedroom not far from the entryway. The door was wide open. He went in.

At the side of the bed, he lowered her feet to the rug. Dizzy with the scent of her, with the taste of her, and the soft, arousing feel of her body so close to him, somehow he still managed to break the incredible kiss.

He knew that they had to be at least a little bit responsible. "I should have thought of this."

"Of what?"

"I don't have condoms…"

She surged up, caught his mouth in a swift, hot kiss, and then sank back to her heels again. "It's okay." She rested her small hands, palms flat, against his chest. "I have them." Her dreamy gaze turned rueful. "I always wanted to be ready, in case it ever felt right with someone. It never did—not in the whole time I've lived in Thunder Canyon. Not until tonight…"

"Well." He ran his palms down the silky skin of her arms. So smooth. And she smelled so good. Like fresh, ripe strawberries and sugared lemons, both at the same time. "Okay, then."

"Just okay?" she teased him.

He chuckled. "Better than okay. Way, way better."

"Then kiss me, Connor." Her eyes were mossy green at that moment, and shining so bright. "Kiss me again…"

He didn't have to be told a third time. He caught her sweet lips and she opened for him, letting his tongue in to play with hers. And as he kissed her, she turned slightly, moving them both around, until the backs of his legs touched the side of the bed.

She guided him, gently pushing him back, until he lay across the tangled white sheets. And she came down with him, soft and sighing, her mouth so wet and sweet. He couldn't get enough of her kisses, couldn't get enough of *her*.

But then she pulled away and rose up on an elbow. She gazed down at him, her lips soft and swollen, her eyes making tempting erotic promises as she tugged on his shirttail, sliding her fingers beneath the knit fabric to caress him.

He groaned at her touch, at the way her soft fingers glided over his flesh, tenderly, teasingly. And he wanted to feel her, all of her, skin to skin. So he sat up, kissed her once, hard and fast, and ripped his shirt up and over his head. Swiftly, he yanked off his boots and got rid of his socks. He undid the button at the top of his fly, and tugged the zipper down. Lifting his hips, he shoved the jeans and his boxer briefs halfway down his thighs.

She helped him, getting hold of the jeans and the briefs, sliding them off the rest of the way, tossing them over the edge of the bed.

At last, he was naked. He felt her gaze on him, sweeping upward over his body to meet his waiting eyes.

She breathed his name on a long sigh. "Connor..." And she swayed against him.

Magic, the feel of her smooth skin pressed to his. He caught her, pulling her close, tucking her tightly to his bare chest, reveling in the silky feel of her hair against his flesh, in the delicacy of her body, the way it curved into his, in the scent of her, so fresh and clean and sweet.

"Tori." Her name sounded so good on his tongue.

She tipped her head back to him with a questioning sound.

"Tori…" He kissed her. And that time, while he kissed her, he touched her, clasping her slim upper arm, palming the firm curve of her shoulder.

Such soft, tempting skin, and all of it his to caress. He traced a finger inward, skimming the bows that held her nightgown in place. And then up, along the velvety skin of her neck, until he reached the heated flutter of her pulse, waiting there for him, in the vulnerable cove at the side of her throat.

He laid his whole hand, flat, against the satiny warmth of her upper chest. Lower still, he curved his fingers around a high, firm breast. She moaned when he did that, and moaned again as he found her nipple through the thin cloth of her nightgown and teased it, rolling it tenderly between his thumb and forefinger.

Those sweet little bows at her shoulders? By then he couldn't resist them. He made short work of them, pulling the end of one and then the other. They fell apart, taking the top of her flimsy little gown down with them.

Her breasts were revealed to him, round and firm, compact, the skin so fine, the delicate blue veins showing faintly beneath. He eased her to her back, bent his head and took her pretty pink nipple into his mouth. She groaned deep in her chest when he did that, and pulled him close to her. He drew on her breast, strongly, and she bowed her slim torso toward him, lifting her breasts, offering him more of her.

The hem of her short gown rode high on her smooth thighs. He reached down, guided it higher.

She wore nothing beneath. He touched her belly, stroking, loving the feel of her, enjoying the eager way she gave herself, so openly, without holding anything of herself away from him. She groaned and clutched his head even tighter to her breast.

And he let his hand wander lower, over the warm silk of her lower belly, to the place where the soft curls were waiting. She lifted toward him, urging him on.

He touched her, dipping a finger into the feminine heart of her. She was wet. Hot. He explored the silky folds and she encouraged him with tender little moans and sighs, as she lifted her hips, opening her thighs to him, so eager. Hungry for more.

So he gave her more. He kissed his way down her body, sliding her gown even higher, until it was no more than a tangled, satin band around her waist. He kissed her belly, dipped his tongue into her navel, and breathed in the musky, sweet scent of her excitement.

He had to taste her. Now. Immediately. He kissed the silky red-gold curls and lower, putting his mouth where his wet fingers had been.

She was writhing by then, her hands clutching his head, fingers speared in his hair, urging him onward. He ran his tongue along the slick wetness, drinking in the taste of her, driving her higher, finding that it aroused him beyond all reason to be giving her pleasure, to know that she liked it, that she wanted him to kiss her in this most intimate way.

And then, all at once, she was crying out his name. She broke, shuddering. He tasted her completion, felt it pulse against his tongue.

Her satisfaction drove him higher, gave him something so good, so right. Something he had never known he craved, something hot and bright and beautiful. Something good and true.

Who knew it could be like this?

Not Connor.

He had never been what anyone would call an attentive lover. With his wife, the sex didn't matter anyway, except for the necessity of producing his son. And with the women he'd dated in the past year, he'd been utterly selfish. He saw that now. They gave him pleasure in the form of sexual release. And he took them out to the best restaurants, showered then with pricey gifts.

But with Tori...

Everything was different.

He got pleasure from *her* pleasure, took satisfaction from knowing she was satisfied.

She sighed, and a little laugh escaped her. "Oh, Connor." Her fingers, now, were gentle in his hair. "Who knew?" Good question. He certainly hadn't. She whispered, "Come up here, up here to me..."

One last press of his lips against those wet red-gold curls and he obeyed her, kissing his way up the middle of her body, over her soft, tempting belly, between her small, perfect breasts. He paused to dip his tongue into the groove at the base of her throat. Never would he get enough of the taste of her, sweet and slightly salty now, with the sweat of their lovemaking.

He kissed her throat, her chin, and finally, with a sigh, he settled his mouth over hers and tasted her more deeply. He was aching, aching in a good way, hard and ready, needing her so bad.

She caught his face in her two soft hands. "The drawer, in the nightstand..."

He reached for it, his mouth still locked with hers.

Finding the knob, he pulled it open, felt around inside, his fingers closing over a pen, a notepad, a small flashlight. But nothing that felt like the condom he was groping for.

She pushed gently at his shoulders. "Let me," she suggested.

Reluctantly, he let her up, and sank back against the pillows. He admired the gorgeous curve of her slim back as she got up on her folded knees and slid the drawer all the way open.

"Got it." She pulled out a box from way in back and swiftly peeled the lid wide, taking out a single sealed pouch. She held it up.

He reached for it.

But she only laughed and snatched it away and looked at him from under her thick lashes. "Let me. Please."

He settled back against the pillow again and folded his hands behind his head. "Absolutely. Be my guest." He spoke teasingly, though he wanted only to grab her, roll her under him and bury himself deep in her waiting softness.

She was kind. She didn't fool around. She had the pouch open and the condom sliding down over him within seconds. The touch of her hand as she guided it into place, snugging it neatly, evenly, at the base, almost undid him.

But not quite. She bent over him, so her lips were no more than a breath away from his. "Good?"

He refused to move. If she wanted to take control, so be it. "Excellent."

She slid a leg over him and went up on her knees astride him, but away from him. Her eyes weren't so teasing anymore. They were hungry. Ready.

He resisted the powerful urge to grab her hips and surge up into her.

She bent close, though she didn't lower herself down onto his waiting hardness. She whispered, "You're gritting your teeth."

"And you're driving me wild."

"I'm so glad to hear that." She kissed him, slowly, a brushing kiss that turned deeper—and then deeper still.

"Come down to me, Tori. Now..."

Impossibly, miraculously, she actually obeyed him. He felt her against him—there, where he needed her—and then he slipped inside.

She was wet and hot and, oh, so welcoming. He couldn't stop himself from reaching for her then. He took her hips and pulled her down onto him.

She moaned then. So did he.

And she rode him, kissing him, her hips working in a rhythm that shattered him, that broke him into a thousand tiny pieces—and then somehow put him back together again.

At the last minute, as he knew he was losing it, he grabbed her more firmly by the round curves of her bottom and he rolled her, so he was on top. She lifted her legs and wrapped them around him, holding him, rocking him, murmuring his name.

He muttered, "Tori," and then again, "Tori," as the world spun away. He saw utter darkness behind his eyes. And then, at the last possible moment, as she turned him inside out, the darkness turned to shimmering light.

They must have slept.

When he woke, the bedside clock said it was almost

five. Tori lay beside him, her face so innocent and sweet
in the light of the lamp they'd left on, her strawberry
hair bright as sunshine spilled across the pillow.

He tried to slide his arm out from under her head
without waking her. But her eyes drifted open.

"Connor…"

"Um?"

"What time…?"

"Five to five."

"You have to go?"

"Unfortunately." He bent close, brushed a kiss on her
forehead. "Tonight I'm going out to the Douglas Ranch.
Caleb invited me to dinner."

She made a low, knowing sound. "More hush-hush
negotiating, huh?"

"We aren't quite at that point yet. Want to come with
me?"

She shook her head. "I think I'll just stay out of that,
if you don't mind."

He kissed the tip of her nose. "Tuesday, then? I'll
take you to dinner."

"I have a better idea."

"What could be better than you, me and dinner?"

"You, me, CJ, Ryan, Jerilyn…and dinner."

He groaned. "Dinner with the kids. Not exactly the
romantic evening I had in mind."

She chided him, "You know it's a good idea."

"Yeah, I suppose it is." He planted a kiss on her sweet
mouth and slid his arm out from under her. "Okay. Tuesday. Dinner with the kids—and I have to go." He jumped
from the bed and grabbed his briefs and his jeans. When
he was fully dressed, he bent close to her for a final kiss.
"Every summer should start this way."

She twined her arms around his neck and lifted her mouth to his. "I couldn't agree with you more."

"You *didn't*." Allaire wore an expression of total disbelief. She sent a quick glance around the Tottering Teapot, clearly worried that someone might have heard what Tori had just said.

"Yeah," Tori answered, after savoring a slow bite of her avocado and swiss sandwich with sprouts. "I did. *We* did. And it was wonderful."

Allaire leaned closer across the lace tablecloth and pitched her voice barely above a whisper. "But you said yourself he admitted he's buying out the resort—and then leaving town."

"I like him. I like him a lot. I want to be with him, for as long as it lasts."

A look of concern crossed Allaire's face. "I just don't want to see you hurt, Tori."

"I know you don't. And I realize that I might be hurt."

"Might?" Allaire demanded.

Tori busted to the truth. "Okay. I guess it's likely, in the end. But I want to be with him more than I want to protect myself against heartbreak. Sometimes you just have to go for it, you know? Go for it and not count the cost."

Connor couldn't stay away from Tori.

She drew him like a bee to a flower, a kid to a cookie jar. He stopped by her house that afternoon and confessed that he couldn't bear to keep away. Tori said she understood completely, that she felt the same.

That night, he went out to the Douglas Ranch, as

planned. Riley Douglas, who was Caleb and Adele's son and Grant Clifton's partner in running the resort, showed up, too. Riley was silent through most of the meal—silent and watchful. When Caleb and Connor discussed the resort, Riley said that he was sure he and Grant could turn things around, given time.

Caleb looked at his son and said in a weary tone, "Money's tight. You know that. And time is the one thing I don't have a lot of."

"Just don't rush into anything," Riley warned.

"I'm not rushing," Caleb replied, sending Connor a telling glance. "I'm considering the options, son. Considering them fully."

When he left the Douglas Ranch, Connor went straight to Tori's. She didn't ask if Caleb had offered to sell him the resort—or anything about what had happened during his visit with the Douglases. He knew she didn't want to know.

And he was more than content to say nothing of his meeting with Caleb. He only wanted to take her in his arms, to feel her soft body pressed close to his.

Tuesday morning after he took CJ and Jerilyn out to Melanie's, he got a call from Grant Clifton. Grant wanted to speak with him alone.

Connor drove up toward the resort, stopping off at the office complex down the mountain from the main lodge. Grant led him to his private office and shut the door.

Grant was furious, Connor could see that in the tightness of his square jaw. He said he'd talked to Riley Douglas that morning.

"Riley clued me in. I get the picture now, and I don't much like what I see. You want the resort and when you get it, people who matter to me, people who have worked hard here, are going to be without their jobs."

"Grant, come on. Let's not get ahead of ourselves."

"I *liked* you," Grant said with deadly softness. "I heard you were here to be with your son, to smooth over past differences with your sister. I admired that. Yeah, I also heard the rumors that you were interested in the resort. I didn't listen to what they said."

"Grant, there's no reason for—"

"You're right." Clifton cut him off. "Getting you here in my office and reaming you a new one isn't a very smart thing for me to do. But I'm just pissed off enough that I don't give a damn what's smart. I just want you to know that *I* know now you're not who I thought you were. You're no better than a vulture, McFarlane. And I wanted to say that to your face."

Connor said nothing. With a curt nod, he turned for the door. Grant made no move to stop him.

As he drove down the mountain, Connor tried to remind himself that he'd been called worse things than a vulture. In the past, he'd never cared. He went after what he wanted and he got it and what people said didn't mean a thing.

Now, strangely, Grant Clifton's harsh words rankled. And he found himself worrying about Melanie and Russ, about their reaction when they learned he had plans for the resort. Tori had warned him he'd better tell Melanie what he was up to.

So he detoured to the Hopping H. He found Melanie in the kitchen, baking cookies. The kids, she said, were out in the barn with Russ.

She took a sheet of great-smelling snickerdoodles from the oven and set them on top of the stove. And

she turned to him. She frowned when she saw his face.
"What? You look like somebody stole your dog."

"I never had a dog."

She chuckled. "Mother never would have allowed
that. 'They are so filthy, darlings.'" She imitated their
mother's cool, aristocratic tones. "'And the shedding.'"
She faked a delicate shudder. "'No. Impossible.'"

He laughed—and then instantly grew serious.
"There's something I need to tell you."

Now she looked worried. Really worried. "What? Is
it about CJ? I think he's doing much better."

"He is. It's not about him."

"Well?"

He laid it on her. "I came here this summer for him.
And to spend some time with you."

"I know that, Connor. And I'm pleased that you're
here."

"And also to buy the Thunder Canyon Resort."

"Yes," she replied. "What else?"

"What do you mean, what else?" he demanded
grimly. "That's it."

"That you want to buy the resort?"

"Yes. I want to buy the resort and I thought you
should know."

She took off the fat oven mitt and waved her hand
airily. "Oh, that. I knew that."

He groped for a chair and lowered himself into it.
"You did?"

"You're my brother, Connor. I know you. I know
how your mind works. The resort is a different type of
property than McFarlane House usually takes on. That
makes it a challenge and you love a challenge. Plus, you

can probably get it for an excellent price. Of course, you'll go after it."

His mouth was hanging open. He snapped it shut. "You knew all along."

"I did. And I knew that you'd tell me about it eventually, when you were ready to discuss it."

He confessed bleakly, "Grant Clifton just called me a vulture."

Her eyes grew sad. "Yes, well. Grant found his calling, managing the resort. It's killing him to watch it fail. I'm sorry to hear he lashed out at you. Please don't take his cruel words to heart. He'll settle down in time. And my guess is that when he does, you'll get an apology."

"But…he and Russ are best friends, aren't they?"

Now her expression was tender. "You're worried about Russ being angry with you?"

"Think about it. Russ and I didn't exactly get off to a great start. I've felt like we're slowly getting on a better footing. But I'm afraid if he gets an earful from Grant, I'll lose all the progress I've made with him."

She sat down at the table with him and put her hand over his. "A girl could do a lot worse than to have a brother like you."

Her words pleased him. Very much. "Thanks. That means a lot."

"It's only the truth."

"Well, lately, at least."

"At least." She chuckled. "And don't worry about Russ. He never liked the resort, thought it brought a lot more growth and questionable 'progress' than Thunder Canyon ever needed. And he always believed that Grant was meant to be a rancher like his father and his father before him. Russ is not going to resent you because Grant might have to consider a career change."

That night, as planned, Tori had Connor and the kids over to her house for dinner. She thought it went well. And she couldn't help but notice that CJ actually looked at his father when he spoke to him.

Plus, there was a new contentment about Jerilyn. She said she liked the job at the Hopping H. And her dad seemed better. The day before, Butch had found a therapist from the list Tori's dad had provided. Insurance would pay the therapist's bill.

"It's a start, I think," Jerilyn told them.

At a little after nine, Connor left with the kids. He would take Jerilyn home. Ryan would come with him and CJ to their house to spend the night. Gerda would take the boys out to the ranch in the morning, stopping to pick up Jerilyn along the way.

Tori stood out on the porch and waved as they drove away, and wished that he would be coming back later to see her alone. But Connor would be leaving first thing in the morning for Philadelphia, gone until Friday evening. She missed him already and wished they'd had a little privacy to enjoy a more intimate farewell.

But then she chuckled to herself. If she'd wanted to be alone with him tonight, she shouldn't have engineered dinner with the kids. She went inside, took a long, hot bath, watched some TV—and wasn't all that surprised when her doorbell rang at ten past twelve.

She didn't say a word. Just held out her eager arms to him.

Connor headed for Bozeman at five the next morning to catch his flight. The trip took longer than it would have in the past. In an effort to cut costs, he flew commercial rather than enjoy the pricey comfort and privacy of a McFarlane House jet.

In Philadelphia, the meetings were endless and both his father and his mother were on his case every chance they got. They wanted him back home. Now. His father argued that the Thunder Canyon Resort was too big for their purposes, too much to take on. McFarlane House had always been a boutique brand. Sprawling resorts—especially failing ones—just weren't a good fit.

Connor listened and nodded. And then reminded them that there was a plan and he was sticking with it, that times were changing and McFarlane House had to change with them.

The flight back was a nightmare. Every plane he boarded had some mechanical issue or other. By late afternoon, he ended up calling everyone—Gerda, CJ and Tori. He told them he would be stuck in an airport hotel in Kansas City for the night. Tori said she missed him. He missed her, too, all out of proportion to the short time he'd been away. CJ asked permission to spend the night at Russ's ranch, the Flying J. One of Russ's mares had just foaled and another was about to. CJ hoped to be there to see the new foal born.

More calls ensued, to Melanie and Russ, who said CJ was welcome to bunk at the Flying J for the night. And that Russ would be glad to drive into town and pick CJ up.

So it was settled. Connor hung up the phone feeling really good. CJ had sounded so excited about the whole thing. More and more, he dared to hope that he was getting his son back, that CJ would move beyond the trauma and pain of his parents' divorce, that he would be okay, after all.

The early flights the next morning, through Denver to Bozeman, went off without a hitch. By a little after ten, he was in his own SUV and on his way back to Thunder Canyon.

At the house, he was alone. Gerda had left a note saying she'd gone for groceries and his lunch was in the fridge. CJ was still out at the Flying J. He hauled his suitcase into his bedroom suite and grabbed the phone to call Tori.

The doorbell rang as he was dialing. He put the phone down and went to answer.

The last person he'd ever expected to see in Thunder Canyon was waiting on the other side. "Jennifer."

She was looking gorgeous, as always, all in white. Her gold hair was streaked with platinum and her skin was a golden brown—no doubt from long, lazy days lounging in the sun on Constantin Kronidis's yacht. At the curb behind her, a gleaming black limo waited.

"Hello, Connor." She pushed her giant, diamond-accented Versace sunglasses up over her forehead and anchored them in her hair. "I need to speak with you."

This was not sounding especially good. But then again, what could she do to him now? The divorce was final, the property divided, custody of CJ settled.

He ushered her inside, into the living room, and gestured for her to sit. She took the sofa. He offered, to be civil, "Can I get you anything?"

She looked up at him, her beautiful face a cold mask. "My son, please."

Last time I checked, he was my son, too, Connor thought. But he kept his mouth shut. The words would only come across as a jab. And at least until he knew what she was up to, he would refrain from antagonizing her.

He sat in the club chair across the coffee table from her. "CJ's out." Instinct had him holding back on telling her where.

Of course, that was her next question. "Out where?"

He cut to the chase. "What do you want, Jennifer?"

She cast a dismissive glance around the room, which was attractive, high-ceilinged and expensively furnished, but certainly not up to her standards of luxury. "Constantin has asked me to marry him."

"Congratulations," he said with reasonable sincerity. "I hope you'll be very happy."

"I'm sure we will. As for CJ, I've changed my mind."

He didn't ask her what she'd changed her mind about. He knew she was going to tell him anyway. He braced himself for the bad news.

And she hit him with it. "On deeper reflection, I don't want my son spending the summer here. It's a waste of his precious time. He's behind in his studies and he needs desperately to catch up. So I've found a fine school in Switzerland, MonteVera, and enrolled him for the summer."

Chapter Seven

Connor sat very still as he resisted the powerful urge to leap across the coffee table, grab his ex-wife by her slim shoulders and shake her until a little warmth and good sense spilled out.

He reminded himself that she *was* the mother of his child. And he hadn't been a good husband to her—in fact, he hadn't been much of a husband at all. She *had* taken good care of CJ in the past. Yes, she'd always been a distant and distracted mother. But she'd been there for CJ when Connor hadn't.

He thought of his own parents, for some reason. His mother had always been a lot like Jennifer. Present, but emotionally unavailable.

His father's voice crept into his mind. *You could just send Connor Jr. back to school. A summer without dis-*

tractions, time to focus on his studies. Do the boy a world of good.

For a moment, he wondered if somehow Donovan McFarlane and Jennifer were in on this thing together.

But then again, no. Jennifer and his parents had never really hit it off. And his father might think he owned the world, but he did have certain principles. Donovan would have considered it unconscionable to scheme against his only son with the woman who had disgraced the McFarlane name by divorcing said son.

"What's the matter, Connor?" Jennifer cooed. "I seem to have struck you speechless."

In a carefully modulated tone, he reminded her, "In case you've forgotten, it was your idea that he spend the summer with me."

She adjusted her sunglasses on top of her head, smoothed a hand down her hair. "Of course I haven't forgotten. But as I said a moment ago, I've rethought the situation. He needs to be closely supervised and this way, he'll have the summer to get on top of his studies and make up for his failure last year. Also, I know he's a burden to you, Connor. And I'm willing to take him off your hands."

"No, thanks."

She blinked her delft-blue eyes. "Excuse me?"

"I think you were right to send him to me. And it's working out well. It's good for him to get to know me, to spend time with his father. And I'm perfectly happy with having him here. He will stay with me. And I'll be more than happy to pay whatever penalties the school in Switzerland demands when you tell them that CJ won't be going there after all."

"This is not about fees, Connor. This is about the welfare of our son."

Our son. Well. Progress. Of a sort. "Yes, it is about CJ's welfare. He and I are getting to know each other this summer. I think you'll agree that it's about time. He seems…happier every day. As to his schoolwork, he's catching up." Okay. Total lie. But Connor would see to it that CJ hit the books, starting immediately.

Jennifer looked pained. "How is he catching up, here, in some nowhere town at the end of the earth?"

The lie reached his lips—and he let it out. "He has a tutor. A very qualified one, as a matter of fact. She teaches at the high school, on the advanced track." Hey, that was partly true, at least. Tori did teach advanced placement English; he knew that for a fact.

"Some country schoolteacher is not good enough. He deserves the best. And MonteVera is world-class." A slight frown creased her satin-smooth brow. "And I don't understand this. I thought you would be pleased to have him taken off your hands."

Two weeks ago, she would have been right. If she'd shown up then to take CJ away, he'd have been only too happy to see his son go. But now…

Uh-uh. Maybe if he was honest with her, straightforward. Okay, it was a novel idea, but it might work.

He leaned toward her, willing her to understand. "Jennifer. The answer is no, he's not going away. The end of August is soon enough for him to go back to school. Try to see his side. He needs this time, here, with me. He's enjoying himself. And he and I…well, when we got here, he would hardly speak to me. That's changing. Slowly. If I send him away now, he won't ever forgive me."

She flipped a thick swatch of that pale hair back over her shoulder, impatient. Thoroughly annoyed. "Connor. Will you listen to yourself? It's always about you, isn't it?"

So much for hoping she might understand. He sat back in his chair, putting as much distance as he could between them while still remaining seated. "I don't think *you* were listening. No, it's not about me. It's about CJ. The divorce has been hard on him."

She huffed, turned her head away, wrapped her arms tightly around herself. "Now you're blaming me."

"No, I'm not. I'm saying he's been hurt enough and he deserves a break. He likes it here in Thunder Canyon and I'm not taking this summer away from him because you've suddenly decided to go back on your own agreements and ship him off to Switzerland."

"I am hardly *shipping* him off. I only want what's best for him."

"Then let him have his summer here."

She shot to her feet. "I want to see him. Now."

"Not until you agree that you won't take him away with you."

"I'll agree to no such thing. What I will do is call my lawyer."

He gazed at her steadily. "Now, you're threatening me?"

She threw up a hand. "You have been a terrible, neglectful father, Connor."

"I could have been better, true. I'm working hard at doing better now."

"You're not hearing me. I'm about to remarry. Constantin can buy and sell you ten times over. I can trample you in court. Do you understand?"

"So, it's all about the money, as always, isn't it, Jennifer?" He said the words wearily. He really didn't want to fight with her. He thought they had both moved on.

Apparently he'd thought wrong.

She drew herself up. "I am telling you to think about it. Take a day or two. And if by Monday morning, you aren't ready to agree to send CJ to Switzerland, I'll be suing you for full custody. And I will win, too."

The last thing he needed right now was another court battle with her, especially considering that she was absolutely right about her fiancé. Kronidis had very deep pockets.

But Connor wasn't going to back down on this. CJ's welfare was at stake. And in the past couple of weeks he'd learned at last that his son—and his son's high regard—meant a lot to him.

"I'll sue you right back," he said icily. "And *I'll* win. Because I'm getting married, as well—to a wonderful, warmhearted woman. A woman who'll be there for CJ, a hands-on kind of mom. A teacher, as a matter of fact— CJ's tutor, whom I mentioned before."

Dear God in heaven, what had he just said?

But the whopping lie was almost worth it—just for the look of stunned shock on his ex's face. Spots of flaming color rode high on those amazing cheekbones of hers. And the blue eyes shot sparks.

He added triumphantly, "Her name is Tori Jones. CJ is crazy about her. Almost as crazy as I am."

Jennifer's sculpted nostrils were flaring. "Oh, you're crazy, all right. You are out of your mind."

"No," he answered with a slow smile. "In fact, I'm saner than I've ever been."

"I seriously doubt that."

He rose. "I think we've said about all we have to say to each other."

If a look could kill, she'd have him dead where he stood. "I'll be back Monday," she said. "Have CJ ready to go. I can find my own way out, thank you."

"CJ is going nowhere." He dropped back to the club chair as she turned for the door.

Once Jennifer was gone, Connor paced the floor, considering his options. They didn't change. It seemed very clear to him what he needed to do next. Too bad it was wrong. And a really big lie.

Not to mention totally unfair to Tori, whom he honestly cared about and had hoped never to hurt.

Still, at this point, he saw no other way out than to call his lawyers and let it go, count on them to fight Jennifer off. Her lawyers were at least as good as his.

And she had Kronidis's billions at her disposal.

No. He was going to fight this every way he could—if it turned out that Tori was willing to help him.

Willing to help him.

Strange. He'd been pacing back and forth for a half an hour, going over the various possibilities, and it had never occurred to him until that moment that he might try lying to Tori, too. That he could propose to her, tell her he'd changed his mind about everything, that he loved her and wanted to marry her and make a home with her, right there in Thunder Canyon. And then when the summer was over, he could plead cold feet and break it off with her.

He almost smiled. First off, she was smarter than that. She would know something wasn't right, for him to flip-flop like that, out of nowhere. Also, she was way too likely to find out about Jennifer and her threats. She'd figure out what he was up to then, for certain.

But even beyond the low probability he could pull it off, he just wasn't willing to lie to her. If she went into this with him, it should be with her eyes wide open.

He called the Flying J. Russ answered and went and got CJ from the barn.

"Dad, hey. You're home."

Home. The way his son said that word…it was everything. The last of Connor's doubts about asking Tori to help him with this fell away. He would do anything to keep CJ where he wanted to be for the whole damn summer.

"I'm here," he said, and meant it in more ways than one. "What's up with the baby horses?"

CJ chuckled. "Foals, dad."

"Right. Foals. Well?"

"Ryan and I are trying to decide on a name for the one born Friday. And the other hasn't come yet. So I was wondering…"

"You want to stay over another night, is that it?"

"Yeah. I was hoping it might be okay."

"What does Russ say?"

"He says it's okay."

In the background, he heard Russ's voice. "Fine with me."

"All right. Until tomorrow morning." They had a few big things to talk about. And they needed to do that before Jennifer came back Monday.

"Okay, Dad. I really gotta go. That foal is coming any minute now, I can just feel it."

Connor murmured a goodbye and heard the click as CJ hung up. He called Tori.

She answered on the first ring. "You're back."

The sound of her voice made his arms ache to hold her. "I want to see you." The words came out low. Rough. Hungry. Not all that surprising, since he *was* hungry. For her.

A low laugh escaped her, a laugh that teased him. "I'm home. Come over right now."

Tori was at the door, waiting for him, when he rang the bell.

She yanked it wide and sighed at the sight of him, so tall, so handsome. Her own personal corporate shark, who had somehow turned out to be the man she longed for. The kind of man she could believe in. She beamed up at him. "I thought you'd never get here."

His dark gaze ran over her, head to toe and back up again. "I know exactly how you feel." And then he reached for her.

She swayed toward him, lifting her mouth for that first, delicious kiss. He covered her lips with his, wrapping his arms good and tight around her, lifting her feet right off the floor, so he could carry her back across her threshold and shove the door shut behind them with his foot.

He kept walking, to the open door just beyond the foyer and right through it. The second he lowered her feet to the rug by the bed, she started tugging on his shirt, unzipping his trousers.

As she undressed him, he did the same for her. He took her camisole top by the hem and pulled it up and off. He undid her shorts and pushed them down. She was naked in no time.

And so was he. They fell across the bed together

rolling, kissing as they caressed each other, each so eager, starving for the simple thrill of the other's hungry touch.

She needed no slow seduction. Not today. Her body was ready for him just from his kiss, from his long, knowing fingers parting her, stroking her. She stuck out a hand and fumbled for the small drawer by the side of the bed.

Since their first time, she'd moved the condoms front and center, with some loose and waiting, outside the box. She grabbed one, broke their endless kiss long enough to rip the top off the pouch with her teeth.

"Now," she whispered to him.

"Oh, yeah…" He rolled them again, so they were on their sides, facing each other.

She reached down between them, loving the hard, hot length of him, as well as the way he moaned when she positioned the condom and rolled it down over him, fitting it smooth and tight.

"Now," he groaned again, and rolled her under him. She opened for him, so ready.

And then he was in her. She wrapped her legs around him. There was only pure sensation, of his body pressed to hers, his hardness filling her, his hips rocking into hers in a rhythm she knew by heart.

She grabbed him closer. She held on so tight. The pleasure bloomed wide, and then contracted in a shimmer of sparks and light.

Her bathtub wasn't that large, but it was big enough for two.

They went in there and filled it and sank into the welcoming heat together. He made his body a cradle for hers and she leaned back against his strong chest and shut her eyes.

"Heaven," she whispered on a sigh. "This, and the rest of it. I love it when you're touching me." His arm, dusted with silky dark hair, rested on the rim of the tub. She ran a wet finger along the strong length of it. "And I love touching you…"

He nuzzled her neck. "It's mutual. Take my word for it." And then he pulled away enough to rest his dark head back on the towel she'd given him to use as a pillow. He was still.

Too still?

Some sharp instinct had her turning to glance over her damp shoulder at him. "Connor?"

"Umm?" He had his eyes closed, his head back, cradled by the towel.

"Is everything…okay?" She wondered why she'd asked that as soon as the words escaped her lips.

But then he sat up straight again and met her gaze levelly.

And she knew that her weird instinct was true. "What is it?"

Suddenly, his eyes were bleak. "I need to ask you something. A…favor. And I'm afraid that when I do, you'll not only say no, you'll ask me to leave. And not to come back."

She moved, then, gripping the tub sides, sloshing water as she turned around to face him. "I think you'd better just ask, then."

"All right. Here it is. I want us to pretend, for the summer, that we are engaged."

She sputtered, "B-but whatever for?"

"Hear me out, okay, before you give me an answer?"

She raked her damp hair back off her forehead. "Okay, then. Explain. And this had better be good."

Chapter Eight

Tori listened, not sure what to think, as Connor told her all of it: the visit from his ex-wife, her demand that he let her send CJ away. Connor's refusal. His ex's threats. His lies—that Tori was tutoring CJ, and that she was his fiancée.

When he was finished, she got out of the bathtub, grabbed a towel and wrapped it around herself. She handed him one, too, and waited as he rose, the cooling bathwater slicking off his fine, hard body.

He dried himself and entered the bedroom, where he pulled on his trousers. She traded her towel for the terry cloth robe that hung on the back of the bathroom door.

They went into the kitchen. Neither of them said a word as she made coffee for him, prepared tea for herself. They both sat at the table.

She sipped her tea. "As to the tutoring. Yes, of course."

"Thank you." He lifted his coffee cup, drank. Set it down.

"But as far as the other…" She felt uncomfortable saying it right out: *pretending to be engaged to him, playing at being his fiancée.* No matter how she chose to put it, it sounded like a foolish thing for two grown people to be doing.

A foolish thing—and a lie.

"As far as the other…" She started again, let the words fade off a second time. She rested her elbows on the table and leaned toward him. "Do you think it's really necessary? I mean, won't the summer be over before she can get any kind of judgment taking him away from you?"

He sipped more coffee. "Legally, she might be able to get some judge to order me to turn CJ over to her within a week or two."

"But don't you share custody? Don't you have as much right to be with your son as she does?"

He looked away—and then faced her again. "It's like this. We share legal custody, but she has physical custody and I have open visitation rights—meaning when I want a weekend with him, I call at least two weeks in advance and she, within reason, has to let me have him, up to a possible total of thirty weekends a year." He set his cup down and turned to gaze blindly out the window again. "That seemed fine with me, at the time of the settlement. I never dreamed I'd want to spend that much time with him, anyway. Frankly, at that point, I wasn't looking forward to the occasional weekend I'd feel duty-bound to take him." Connor continued to stare out the window. Even in profile, she could see how disgusted he was with himself.

She had to actively resist the need to reach across, to cover his hand with hers. "But then Jennifer guilted you into taking him for the summer..."

He looked at her again. "And I've slowly discovered I want to be a real dad, after all."

She reminded him, "CJ's fifteen. Isn't that old enough to have a say in this? You *are* going to tell him what's going on, won't you?"

He nodded. "He's at the Flying J overnight. Tomorrow, when I pick him up, I'll talk to him about it. Find out for sure what *he* wants."

"If he wants to stay—which I'm guessing he will—that should be enough, shouldn't it, to sway any judge? That a fifteen-year-old boy should get the summer with his father, the summer that his mother set up in the first place?"

"I'm hoping it won't come to CJ having to face a judge over something that was supposed to have been settled already."

"To...choose sides between you and his mother in court, you mean?"

"That is exactly what I mean. I just want to give him—give both of us—this summer we didn't even know that we needed. I don't want to lose the ground I've gained with him. And if she gets a judge to order me to let her take him away...well, he's been making real progress. His attitude about me, about life...about himself, really—it's all so much better. He even seems *happy* at times lately, you know? I don't think I can bear to let Jennifer snatch that away from him."

Tori looked down into her teacup, but found no

answers there. "I'm still not sure that pretending I'm your fiancée is going to help you with this."

"You're a respected schoolteacher. You're likable. A good person. The kind of woman who would be the perfect stepmother for him, an ideal choice for my wife. If I can tell my lawyers that you're going to marry me, going to help me provide the kind of home CJ will thrive in when he's with us, and that's why I've decided to sue for joint custody, they should be able to hold the line on Jennifer until at least the end of August."

Hold the line, she thought. *He wants to hold the line.* He thought that she, Tori, would make the perfect wife and mother. But he still wasn't offering to make it real between them. He wanted to play at being married, just long enough to keep his ex at bay.

Oh, it would be so easy to get angry with him now.

But no. She had known who he was, what he was and wasn't capable of, when she decided to snatch this one beautiful summer with him. She refused to suddenly start expecting more of him than he was willing to give.

"Connor. Has it occurred to you that maybe your lawyers can hold the line anyway, without me having to pose as your fiancée?"

"Yeah. It's occurred to me. But I'm willing to play every angle I've got to keep my son where he wants to be, to make sure he gets his summer in Thunder Canyon. If I let Jennifer send him away now, I'll lose what progress I've made trying to show him that I want to be a real father to him. I can't afford that. *He* can't afford that."

When he said it that way, she wanted to say yes, to

promise she would be his pretend fiancée if he needed her to, to do *anything* to help him and CJ.

And yet…

"What about when the summer's over?"

He sighed. "Frankly, Tori, I'm not looking that far ahead."

"Don't you think maybe you should?"

After a moment, he nodded. "Yeah. All right. When the summer's over, we would…break up. It does happen, you know."

"And *then* what about your custody arrangement?"

"I'm hoping I'll have joint physical custody by then. And I *am* CJ's father. Once I have joint custody, it's going to be very hard for Jennifer to convince a judge to take it away."

"You think you can settle a custody battle in two months?"

"I don't know. Maybe not. But I can keep Jennifer from sending CJ away for that long. With your help, I know I can keep CJ here, where he wants to be, until school starts. With your help, I'll have two months to prove to my son that I really do intend to be a father to him."

Tori got up, went to the counter, got a fresh tea bag and poured more hot water over it. She purposely kept her back to him the whole time.

Finally, she turned to him. "I can't make this decision today. I need a little time to think about it. And I think you need to talk with CJ, make absolutely certain that he actually wants what we're both so sure he does."

"I understand." He pushed his coffee cup away and rose. "I have to know your answer by tomorrow, so I can call my lawyers first thing Monday morning."

She picked a random deadline out of the air, because he needed one—and because she did, too. "Tomorrow afternoon."

"Two o'clock?"

"I'll be here."

After Connor left, the house seemed emptier than usual. Tori ran a load of laundry, dusted the living room, changed the sheets on the bed. The simple, everyday actions brought her no closer to having a decision to offer Connor.

She hoped that by the morning, she'd have made up her mind.

Allaire called at a little after three and invited her over for dinner that night. "I mean, if you haven't got a hot date with you-know-who…" Allaire's voice was teasing, free of any hint of judgment. Whatever her private opinion of Connor, she wasn't going to put him down while Tori was going out with him.

Tori wondered wryly what her friend would say if she announced tomorrow that she and Connor were engaged.

"I would love to come. What time should I be there and what can I bring?"

"That yummy salad you make with the mandarin oranges and roasted pecans. Six?"

"I'm there, on time, with the salad."

The evening was a good one. Dinner was delicious and Tori got to help tuck Alex into bed. Later, she considered confiding in her best friend.

But she dismissed that idea about a minute after she thought of it. Allaire would tell her she was crazy to even consider such a thing, that perpetrating a big, fat lie would do no good for anyone—and likely cause everyone involved a world of hurt.

Plus, well, whatever Allaire's reaction might be to the news that Connor had asked Tori to pose as his bride-to-be, it just wasn't right to tell her. It wasn't right to tell *anyone*. Connor had confided in her, put his trust in her. She would not betray that trust, whatever decision she made come tomorrow afternoon.

Before Tori left for the twenty-mile drive home from the small ranch Allaire and DJ owned, Allaire asked her if she had something on her mind. Tori put on a bright smile and lied through her teeth.

"Nope. Not a thing. Thanks. It was a good evening." She hugged her friend, said good-night to DJ, grabbed her empty salad bowl and took her leave.

At home, she turned on all the lights in spite of the waste of electricity. But pushing back the shadows did little to banish her apprehensions. So she turned most of them back off again and she stayed up until after two watching movies she'd already seen before.

There was something so comforting about knowing how it would all come out in the end.

At ten the next morning, Connor collected CJ at the Flying J. CJ talked steadily through the whole drive back to the house in New Town. The second foal had been born, though they'd had to call the vet since the foal was breech and Russ couldn't get it to turn.

"Dad. It's gross. But kind of amazing, you know? Uncle Russ just stuck his arms inside that mare, past his elbows, and tried to turn that foal around. And the vet did the same thing—and it worked that time. The foals are so cute, little spindly legs, and those great big eyes."

Connor glanced over at his son. "So you had a good time, huh?"

CJ grunted. "Dad, I had a *great* time."

Connor decided to wait till they were at the house to discuss Jennifer's demand.

But as soon as they got there and got CJ's duffel and pack inside, CJ announced, "I have to call Jerilyn," and disappeared into his room.

Connor waited. A half an hour later, CJ was still in his room with the door shut. He waited another fifteen minutes before he tapped on the door.

"Yeah?"

Connor turned the doorknob and stuck his head in. His son was sprawled on the bed, the phone to his ear.

"Hold on," CJ said, and took the phone away from his ear. "Dad, can I go over to Jerilyn's?"

Why not? "Sure, but I need a minute or two first. There's something we should discuss." He tried to sound easy and casual, not to get CJ upset before they'd even started talking.

But the kid must have picked up something. "What's wrong?"

Connor put on a smile. "Tell Jerilyn hi for me and say you'll be over soon. Then we'll talk."

Not sixty seconds later, CJ joined him in the living room. He dropped to the sofa. "So...what's up?"

Connor, in the club chair across the coffee table— the same chair he'd sat in when Jennifer laid down her ultimatum—had no idea how to begin this conversation, though he'd been rehearsing it in his head since he left Tori's house the day before.

"Dad?"

Connor sucked in a breath—and laid it right out there. "Your mother came here yesterday. She came to pick you up. She's arranged for you to spend the summer at the MonteVera School in Switzerland. She wants you to get a chance to focus on your schoolwork, to get caught up for next term."

CJ said a very bad word, followed by a single syllable in the negative. "No."

"I'm going to ignore the swearing in this situation."

"Gee, Dad. Thanks." CJ ladled on the sarcasm. And then he asked, with more hope than anger, "What did you tell her?"

"I told her absolutely not. That we had an arrangement already in place for the summer and I intended to stick with it, that you were enjoying your stay here in Thunder Canyon and I saw no reason to send you to Switzerland."

CJ's face lit up. The sight not only tugged at Connor's heartstrings, it also made him all the more certain he'd called it right in this case. "You did? You said that?"

Connor nodded. "And I put her off, refused to tell her where to find you. I wanted to get this chance to speak with you first."

CJ spread his knees, braced his elbows on them and linked his hands between them. "Good. That's good."

"I wanted to be certain that you really want to stay here for the summer."

"Are you kidding me?" CJ bounced on the couch cushions, unable to contain himself. "Of course I do."

"You should be sure. If you do stay, your mother has threatened to take legal action."

CJ made a scoffing sound. "Oh, right. Suddenly she gives a crap."

"CJ, I'm sure she's doing what she thinks is best." Actually, he wasn't sure. But she *was* CJ's mother and as such he refused to let CJ disparage her.

"She doesn't care what's best for me, Dad. She cares about her new boyfriend and his big boat and all his money."

Connor just looked at him, levelly. "CJ. Stop."

CJ's red-brown hair, still badly in need of the services of a good barber, fell over his eyes as he stared at the floor between his knees. "You mean it? You'll tell her you want me with you, that I'm here for the summer the way that we said from the first?"

"Yes. I mean it. I will tell her—I've already told her—that you're staying, that we're sticking with the original plan."

"Well, okay." CJ glanced up, shoved the hair out of his eyes. "Thanks."

"Don't thank me yet. She said she'll be back Monday to get you."

"But she's *not* getting me, right, she's not sending me away?" He looked so worried that Connor would let him down. And why wouldn't he be worried? Connor had been letting him down almost since the day he was born.

"No." Connor spoke slowly. Clearly. "You're staying here, as we agreed. And when she comes tomorrow, you'll have to be here, you'll have to speak with her."

"Why?"

"CJ, she can't only hear this secondhand, from me. She needs to hear it from you. You have to tell her what *you* want."

CJ stared. And then he shook his head. His hair fell over his eyes again. But then, at last, he shoved it back and nodded. "All right. I will. Whatever."

"When you tell her, you'll do it respectfully, please."

"Yeah. Okay. Respectfully."

"And there's another thing…"

"What else?"

"Since your mother was concerned about your wasting the summer without making any effort to catch up on your studies, I told her that Tori was tutoring you."

CJ's eyes grew wide. "You lied."

If his son only knew. "I did. Since then, I've discussed the problem with Tori. She's agreed to help. If you stay, you'll have to be willing to turn my lie into the truth. You'll have to work with Tori, every day, five days a week, starting Monday. And you'll have to do the assignments she gives you. With your job at the Hopping H and the time you'll need to put in on your studies, the summer will be a busy one."

"Ms. Jones will tutor me…" He seemed to consider the idea.

"Yes, she will. And you will have to work hard on the school stuff, no slacking. I need that agreement from you."

CJ looked down between his spread knees again. And when he glanced up, it was to give a firm nod. "You got it, Dad. I'll study with Ms. Jones."

"This will be your opportunity to prove to your mother, and to me—and most of all, to yourself—that you don't need to go to Switzerland to get your studies back on track."

"And I will prove it, Dad."

Connor made a low, approving sound. "I believe that you will."

"Thanks, Dad. I really mean that." The look in CJ's eyes said it all.

They had come a long way, the two of them. Connor was more determined than ever to make this the summer when he healed the past wounds he'd inflicted on his innocent son.

Ten minutes later, CJ was out the door, on his way to see Jerilyn. He'd been invited to her house for lunch, but he promised he'd be back home for dinner.

After he left, Connor called Melanie to explain that CJ's mother was coming by sometime Monday morning, so CJ would be late for work in order to have a little time with her. Melanie said it was no problem. And Russ or Butch Doolin would see that Jerilyn got a ride out to the ranch.

Then she said, in a tone that managed to be simultaneously cautious and offhand, "I thought Jennifer was in Europe for the summer."

"Yeah," Connor answered bleakly. "So did I."

Melanie was quiet for a moment, before asking gently, "Something going on?"

"It's a long story."

"I'd like to hear about it if you feel like telling me."

He surprised himself by doing exactly that. He told her all about Jennifer's visit. And about the conversation he'd just had with CJ. He told her that Tori would be tutoring CJ for the summer.

Yes, he left a gap. A big one. He failed to mention the part about how he'd told Jennifer that Tori was his fiancée. And since he didn't mention that particular whopper of a lie, there was no need to explain how Tori was still deciding whether to pretend to be engaged to him or not.

When he was finished, Melanie said she was proud of him. "I know it means the world to CJ, that you're sticking by him, that now he's found out he likes it here, you're keeping your word about this summer."

"Yeah. It's kind of funny. If you'd told me three weeks ago that CJ would be working at the Hopping H and was willing to study hard with a tutor in order to be allowed to stay in Thunder Canyon with me for the summer, I would have said you were out of your mind."

"He was angry at you, acting out. But deep down, what he really wanted, even then, was to be here, with you—and to know that you wanted him with you."

"Maybe. But now I do know, for certain, that he wants to be here. He's said so himself."

"And you're going to fight for him."

"Yes. I am."

Tori's doorbell rang at two on the dot.

Her pulse suddenly on hyperdrive, she went to answer. "Hello, Connor." He looked so serious, and handsome enough to break a thousand hearts. She wanted to fling herself into his strong arms, to swear she would do anything he wanted, anything to help.

Somehow, she managed *not* to throw herself at him. He didn't reach for her, either. She ushered him in.

She still had no idea what to say to him. Should she go with the passionate urging of her foolish heart and tell him that, yes, she'd be only too happy to be his fake fiancée for the summer? Or did she refuse to help him in this lie—and in the process, end up helping his ex to hurt him *and* CJ?

They ended up sitting at either end of her couch. Once they were both settled, there was a silence. An excruciating one.

Finally, he spoke in low, restrained tone. "I talked with CJ this morning."

"And?"

"He said he wants to stay here for the summer. He wants it very much. He's agreed to study with you, to be guided by you and to do his homework faithfully."

"Great."

"I was thinking, Monday through Friday, in the afternoon—say, two to four? And then homework for him, to amount to a couple of hours five nights a week."

"That sounds fine with me," she said. "I'd be happy to do it."

He named an hourly rate that was higher than she would have asked and added, "Starting Monday?"

"Yes. The rate will be fine and I can start Monday."

"Whatever you think, Tori. You know what you're doing."

As a teacher? Yes, she did.

As a woman and potential phony fiancée?

Not so much.

More silence. She had no idea where to begin. Apparently, neither did he.

Finally, she ventured, staring straight ahead and not at him. "People could be hurt if we did it."

He didn't ask what *it* was. He knew as well as she did. She glanced his way and saw him looking at the far wall. She watched as he shrugged. "That's how life is. Sometimes you get hurt."

"I don't mean just you and me. CJ, too. He could get hurt. He could get his hopes up."

He turned to her, then. A frown creased his brow. "About?"

"You and me, making a permanent home, here. In Thunder Canyon. Since he likes it here so much, he could decide he wants to live with us."

Connor was still frowning. "So we'll just tell him we haven't decided how we're going to work out the details of where to live, of where our home base will be. That we're playing it all by ear and the only thing we do know is that he will go back to his boarding school in the fall."

She chided, "He could still be hurt when it doesn't work out."

"Not as much as he'll be hurt if I let Jennifer send him to Switzerland."

She happened to agree with him on that. "If we did it, we would have to agree to tell no one else. No one. Not Melanie."

He was on the same page with that. "And not your friend Allaire."

"That's right. No one."

"No one," he echoed, in the tone of a man swearing a solemn oath.

Her pulse had started knocking again, her heart beating so hard against the wall of her rib cage. It was time to decide. She needed to tell him—yes or no. They were both facing front again.

She slid him another glance. "It would have to look

real. Which means you would have to propose, so I would have a proposal story to tell."

"A proposal story?"

"Yes." *Men,* she thought. "A woman will always tell her proposal story—where they were when he proposed, what he said, if he went down on his knees. If we want to be believed, I've got to have my proposal story."

He cleared his throat. "Fair enough. I'll make sure you have one."

"And a ring. There would have to be a ring. I would help you pick it out. And, of course, I would return it when things…don't work out."

"A ring," he repeated. "Absolutely." They were looking at each other again. In a voice barely above a whisper, he asked, "Well, then?"

She swallowed, hard. And nodded. "Then yes, all right. I will be your fake fiancée for the summer."

He blinked. "You just said yes. Tell me you just said yes."

"Yes."

He stared, unmoving, for several heartbeats.

And then, without further prompting, he got up, picked up the coffee table and moved it out of the way— and he got down on his knees.

She giggled, a silly, girlish sound. At the same time, tears blurred her vision. "Oh, Connor."

He took her hand, kissed the back of it, gazed up at her through dark eyes suddenly filled with light. It could have been real. And she couldn't help herself. She wished that it was.

"Tori, you are the most amazing woman I have ever met. I love everything about you—the sound of your laughter, the beauty of your smile. Your strawberry hair and the cute freckles on your nose."

She groaned. "You just *had* to mention the freckles."

He put a hand to his heart. "Yes. I love those freckles. Because they're yours. I love all of you, every inch. I love the way your lips feel when they're pressed to mine. I love the way you sigh when I touch you, the way you moan when I—"

She put up a hand.

"What?" He pretended to scowl.

She gazed down at him adoringly. "You can be so romantic."

"Thanks. I'm trying."

And then she shook a finger at him. "But don't get overly graphic, okay? A proposal story should be G-rated, PG if you must, but that is really pushing it."

"Yes. All right. G-rated. I understand." And then he kissed her hand again and pressed it to his heart. "Marry me, Tori. Please. I love you. Say you'll be mine."

She beamed. "Excellent."

He prompted, "Well?"

And she gave him her answer. "Oh, Connor. I love you so much. With all my heart. Yes, of course, I'll marry you."

He swept to his feet, dragging her up with him and he wrapped her tightly in his arms. "Right answer," he whispered against her lips.

"So glad you liked it. As far as the lead-in—"

"The lead-in?" He lifted his head and scowled at her.

"Yeah. We need a lead-in. Meaning, what made you decide to propose today?"

"Ah. Well, I…was away for three days. I missed you unbearably. I knew the minute I saw you again, I'd be on my knees. And I was."

"Wow. That's good."

He was the soul of modesty. "I kind of thought so."

"Except that it doesn't add up. I mean, you saw me yesterday, after your trip."

"Okay, then. How's this? I waited a day, though it was hell for me, just to make certain I couldn't live without you."

She laughed. "Connor. Get outta here. You're *really* good at this."

"I do my best." He brought his lips down so close to hers again.

She could drown in those dark eyes of his. She whispered, prayerfully, "You should kiss me now."

"My thoughts, exactly." He claimed her lips in a kiss that stole the breath from her body and made stars dance behind her eyes.

And then, their mouths still fused, he scooped her high against his chest and turned for her bedroom.

That was when the doorbell rang.

They groaned in mutual disappointment and he whispered, "Get rid of whoever it is. Do it fast."

She chuckled. "You're so eager. I like that in a fiancé, even a fake one."

"Just answer the door," he growled as he let her slide to the floor. She straightened her shirt, smoothed her hair and went to see who it was.

"Hey, Ms. Jones," Jerilyn and CJ chimed in unison when she opened the door. Both were grinning, wind-blown and pink-cheeked.

CJ added, "We were just riding by…" He tipped his

head toward the front walk, where his skateboard and Jerilyn's bike lay as they'd dropped them. "We saw my dad's SUV…"

"Come on in." She stepped back and called to Connor. "It's the kids." They trooped in. "Thirsty?"

Jerilyn laughed. "We were hoping you would ask."

"There's juice in the fridge."

"Thanks, Ms. Jones."

"Hey, Dad," CJ greeted his father as he went by.

Tori went to stand beside Connor as the kids disappeared into the kitchen. They heard cupboards opening, the clunk of the icemaker, followed by cheerful clattering sounds as ice cubes dropped into glasses.

Connor wrapped an arm around her, nuzzled her hair. "I guess it wouldn't be nice to tell them to get lost."

She laughed. "They won't stay long."

CJ appeared carrying a glass of juice. "You guys look…happy."

Connor squeezed her shoulder and captured her gaze. "Good a time as any, don't you think?"

She felt like a diver, poised, suspended in that last split second before she sailed off a cliff into dangerous deep waters far below. But the decision was made. She took the plunge. "Yes. I think so."

By that time, Jerilyn, with her own full glass, had come to stand with CJ. "A good time for what?"

Connor squeezed her shoulder again. "We want you two to be the first to know."

The teenagers shared a bewildered glance. And CJ asked, "Know what?"

Connor announced with pride, "That Tori has just agreed to be my wife."

Chapter Nine

For a moment, Connor worried that CJ was angry, that he hated the idea of his dad planning to marry again. The two kids just stood there, gaping.

And then Jerilyn gave a gleeful laugh. "How great."

And CJ let out a whoop. "Score!"

Connor blinked, unsure. "Uh. That's good, right?"

"Totally, Dad. Sweet," CJ confirmed.

Jerilyn came rushing over. She set her drink on the coffee table and grabbed Tori. "Oh, I'm so happy." She pulled her favorite teacher close, hugging hard. "You're perfect for him, Ms. Jones. I knew it right from the first."

Tori hugged her back. "Um, you did?"

Jerilyn took her by the shoulders and held her away, beaming at Tori with complete satisfaction. You would have thought CJ's girlfriend had engineered the engagement herself. "Well, maybe not that *first* day." She sent a glance at Connor. "That first day, you were kind of scary, Mr. McFarlane."

Connor felt a little abashed. "Yeah. I suppose I was. Sorry."

"But up at the summer kickoff barbecue. That was when I got the feeling you guys might get together."

Now Tori laughed. "No."

"Oh, yeah." She grabbed Tori's left hand. What was it about women? Even the really young ones went right for the ring finger. "Wait. Where's the ring?"

Tori blinked. "Well, um, we…"

On the fly, Connor came up with an answer. "I couldn't wait to ask her. And we've just agreed to drive over to Bozeman today and choose one."

"Wow, Dad," said CJ. He actually looked a little misty-eyed. "This is pretty cool."

Looking at him, Connor could almost feel guilty for deceiving him like this—but not that guilty. After all, he was doing what he had to do, to keep CJ with him.

"So when's the wedding?" Jerilyn demanded.

Tori shook her head. "Slow down, we just got engaged. Let us enjoy the glow for a while before we start in about the wedding."

CJ said, "Hey. So are we moving here, for good, then, Dad? That would be so sweet. If we lived here, I could go to Thunder Canyon High."

Connor felt a shiver down his backbone. Already his son was dreaming of a future in Thunder Canyon—a future that was never going to happen. "We've made no plans yet. None. Enjoy the summer, CJ. Leave it at that."

"I will, Dad. But if you're—"

Connor didn't let him finish. "CJ."

CJ hesitated. But he didn't exactly give up. "Well, we can talk about it later, huh?"

Connor knew he had to draw the line on this or he'd never hear the end of it. "You will go back to boarding school, as always." He spoke flatly. "I can get you your summer, CJ, even though your mother wants it otherwise. But you can't push me beyond that."

CJ stared at the floor. Finally, he sighed. "Okay, Dad."

Connor nodded. "Good, then." Tori and Jerilyn were looking uncomfortable. In Tori's hazel eyes, he saw again all the ways their fake engagement could cause more problems than it would solve. He put on a cheerful tone. "So. You two want to come with us, to pick out the ring? We can all go out to dinner afterward."

Jerilyn was already shaking her head. "Oh, no. You guys have to do that alone."

Connor laughed. "What? That's some kind of requirement?"

"Well, yeah. It's a totally romantic moment, choosing a ring. You don't need us there for that."

Connor happened to glance at CJ, who made a big show of shrugging and shaking his head. "Don't ask me. I know nothing about that stuff."

Jerilyn held firm. "*I* do. You two should choose the ring together, just the two of you." And she added with a glowing smile, "Plus, well, my dad and I are having dinner together tonight. Sunday dinner, as a family, we both agreed."

So it was decided that the teenagers would continue with their afternoon, as planned. And Tori and Connor would make a quick trip to Bozeman.

Ten minutes later, the kids were on their way to Main Street and the park nearby and Tori and Connor were in the SUV, headed out of town.

She sent him a glance across the console. "Just think. If we weren't pretending to be engaged, we could be having wild sex right now. Instead, we're off to buy a ring that will probably cost you a whole lot more than you want to spend."

He held her gaze for an extra second before turning his eyes back to the road. "This won't take long at all. I think we can fit in the wild sex when we get back to your house."

She tried to stifle a laugh. "Oh. Well. I'm so relieved to hear that."

"I knew you would be. And as to the ring, whatever it costs, you're worth it."

She chuckled, and then grew serious. "You realize, don't you, that already CJ's imagining his new life here in Montana—year-round?"

"I made it clear to him that he's going back to school."

She spoke softly. "I know you did. But that doesn't mean you've heard the last of it from him. Now he's got it in his head that you might make a permanent home here in town, he's going to keep trying to get you to agree that he should live here with you."

He captured her hand, brought it to his lips. "It's going to work out fine. You'll see."

"I sincerely hope so."

They found a jewelry store that was not only open on Sunday, it also had a really nice selection of engagement diamonds.

As Connor expected she might, Tori tried to choose something inexpensive and plain.

He wouldn't let her. "Don't forget my rep as a rich corporate shark—I say that one." The ring he indicated had a giant princess-cut stone surrounded by lots of tiny pavé diamonds. More pavé diamonds, channel-cut, glittered in the platinum band.

Tori's eyes lit up. "Oh, that's much too extravagant."

Connor sent the jeweler a wry smile. "She wants to try it on."

"Yes, of course." The jeweler beamed back at him, dollar signs shining in his eyes.

"Connor. No. Really."

"Now, now." The jeweler clucked his tongue. "You must at least try it on." He winked at Connor as he took her hand and slid the gorgeous rock onto her finger. "Ah. Yes. It's beautiful on you. Just exquisite."

"She loves it," Connor said. "We'll take it."

"Oh, Connor—"

He didn't even let her get started. "No more discussion. It's settled." He passed the jeweler his credit card.

Tori looked down at the ring—and then up at him again. "I knew you would do this. You are much too extravagant. You realize that, don't you?"

He framed her face. "Not extravagant in the least. My perfect bride deserves the perfect ring."

And then he kissed her. She smiled against his lips and for a moment or two, he almost found himself believing that they really were a couple in love, that the ring on her finger meant the start of a lifetime—*their* lifetime, together.

But it didn't, of course. And he needed to remember that.

Tori tried not to spend the whole drive home admiring the ring.

She tried to remember that the ring might be real, but the engagement wasn't. That the gorgeous diamond he'd just put on her finger was only for show and she would be returning it at the end of August. That she must keep her head, above all. Not get too attached. To the ring.

Or to him.

At her house, he shut and locked the front door behind them. And then he took her in his strong arms, claiming her mouth in a kiss that lasted forever and made her doubts fly away. He peeled off her clothes and his own, leaving a trail of shirts and shoes and jeans and underwear as he waltzed her backward to her bedroom door.

By the side of bed, he clasped her bare shoulders and guided her down so she sat on the edge. Holding her gaze, he sank to his knees.

With tender hands, so gentle and slow, he eased her thighs apart. And he kissed her, deeply, there at the heart of her womanhood, a long, wet, lovely kiss, a kiss that was so intimate, it was almost beyond bearing.

But, oh, she did bear it. She reveled in it. She clutched his dark head, her fingers buried in the silky strands of his hair. And she offered herself, shamelessly, completely, without holding back.

When her climax rushed over her, he went on kissing

her, drawing the last drop of pleasure from the sweet, endless pulsing, making the fulfillment go on and on.

And then, after that, when he rose up above her and came down across the white sheets with her, she lay dazed and limp beneath his expert caresses, only wanting more of him. Wanting everything.

All he would give her.

All the pleasure, all the excitement, all the pure joy they would share in this too-brief summer allotted to them.

He kissed her breasts, her belly. And then slowly, his soft lips trailed back up again, along the center of her body. He kissed her throat, scraped his teeth along the curve of her chin. And then, at last, he claimed her mouth. She tasted her own desire on his lips, musky and hot.

Consumed by his burning kiss, she was vaguely aware that he reached out and pulled open the drawer in the nightstand. He lifted his mouth from hers.

She groaned and tried to pull him back.

He whispered, "Wait…"

Wait?

She did not want to wait.

With another groan—one of protest, this time, she opened her eyes. And understood.

With amazing, swift dexterity, he had a condom out and ready. He rolled it down over himself.

"Now?" she whispered on a pleading note.

He granted her a slow smile. "Now."

"Come here, then. Hurry." She moaned again, reaching for him, tugging at his hard shoulders, urging him to come to her.

And he did, he covered her, all corded muscle and

burning heat. She reached down between them, encircling him, loving the way he groaned against her lips when she touched him, when she guided him into her, lifting her body up, offering him everything.

He took what she gave, took *her.* And she was ready, so wet and eager. Primed to accept him. He slid in as though he were made for her, made to be with her.

When he moved, she went with him, taking the cues his body gave her, answering back in kind. Wrapping her legs around his lean hips, holding on so tight, she felt for a moment that they were one body, so fully joined there was no separating them.

She cried out when she reached the finish, her body pulsing around him. And he joined her. They rode the wave of completion together. The whole world narrowed down to a hot pinpoint of searing light and pleasure. She rode the light, up and over, to the edge of fulfillment, and then finally over, with a long sigh, into limp satisfaction.

Connor relaxed, too, on top of her. They were both sweating, breathing hard. She kept her arms and legs wrapped around him for the longest time, wishing she would never have to let him go.

He didn't want to leave her. But it was almost five.

Reluctantly, he eased his body to the side. He kissed her sweat-damp shoulder. "I have to go…"

She touched his hair, brushed a finger over his cheek. "I know."

"Want to have dinner at my house with me and CJ?"

She lifted up on an elbow and braced her head on her hand. Her face was sweetly flushed. Even the freckles on her nose were slightly pink. And her strawberry hair was wild, tangled.

He thought he'd never seen anyone so sexy in his life.

"It's tempting," she said. "But you two need a little guy time now and then. You've been gone most of the week."

He leaned close, stole one last quick kiss. "I guess you're right."

She frowned. "But I was thinking…"

"About?"

"Tomorrow. You said your ex-wife was coming, supposedly to pick up CJ, in the morning."

"Yeah."

"Do you want me to be there?"

He chuckled. And not really with humor. "You think you're up for that? Jennifer can be a complete bitch when she's not happy about a situation."

"It's okay. I can take it. I'm a teacher, remember? I'm used to smiling sincerely no matter what, staying diplomatic and upbeat in the most uncomfortable situations. And, well, if I met her, she and I might just hit it off. Maybe she would rethink her unreasonable demands."

"Seriously, Tori. You don't know Jennifer."

"In any case, it wouldn't hurt for her to see that I really exist and I'm relatively harmless, would it?"

Actually, he thought it was a great idea. At least in theory. "If you're volunteering, I'm more than happy to accept the support. But I warn you, it could get ugly."

"I can take it."

He kissed her again. "And you have to promise that no matter what she says to you, no matter how rude she is, you won't let her change your mind about you and me."

She put on a very solemn expression. "I promise, Connor. I will be your bogus fiancée until the end of August, no matter what your ex-wife does tomorrow morning."

"Excellent." He kissed her again and wished he could linger.

But she pulled away. "Go on, now. Have your evening with CJ."

He dragged himself up and out of her bed. Then he followed the trail of clothing that led out toward the entry area, separating his from hers and getting dressed as he went.

She pulled on a robe and joined him at the door. "What time tomorrow?"

"Jennifer didn't give an exact time. Just another of her techniques to keep everyone off-balance. Be there at nine?" He waited for her nod. "I'll call you if she shows up earlier than that."

CJ was already at the house when Connor arrived. They had dinner together. CJ talked about Jerilyn, about his job at the Hopping H.

"I got paid Friday," he announced with pride.

Connor gazed across the table at him and felt real satisfaction at their progress in the past few weeks. His son *was* doing better. And he was also growing up.

It wouldn't be too many more years before CJ was old enough to make his own decisions, about his future. About the kind of life he wanted to lead.

And it was Connor's job to make sure CJ had the tools and abilities he needed to enjoy a successful, productive, reasonably happy adult life.

"When will you and Ms. Jones get married?" CJ wanted to know.

"We haven't decided yet."

"Did you get her a ring?"

"Yes, I did."

"Is it a nice one?"

"I think so. And she seems pleased with it."

"Well, Dad. Cool."

"After dinner, I was thinking we would look through the books you brought with you, kind of get you focused on your studies again, review what you see as your strengths, where you're caught up. And where you need work."

CJ groaned. But it was a good-natured sound. "Do we have to?"

"It'll give Tori a starting point for your first tutoring session tomorrow."

CJ ate a big bite of the meat loaf Gerda had prepared for them. He chewed and swallowed, took a gulp of his milk and set the glass down firmly. "Yeah. I think you're right, Dad. Something to start with. That would be a good thing."

They worked for three hours that night, going through the schoolbooks from the year before, marking the points where CJ needed more work. They went online and got copies of his grades, so that Tori could see which classes he was weak in.

At ten, they knocked off. CJ put the books away and then came to sit next to Connor on the end of the bed.

"Dad? Do I *have* to be here when Mom comes tomorrow?"

Connor completely understood his son's apprehension.

But there was no getting out of dealing with Jennifer—for either of them. "Yeah. You need to talk to her. You need to tell her how you feel, what you want."

CJ made a low sound. "Like she'll listen."

"Respectfully," Connor reminded him.

"I know, Dad. I remember."

Connor wanted to hug him. But he'd never been physically demonstrative with CJ. Would it freak the kid out if suddenly Connor started with the hugs?

It kind of freaked Connor out, to think about it.

He settled for firmly clasping his son's shoulder. "It'll be fine."

CJ snorted. "Come on, Dad. You know Mom. She wants things her way, always has. It's not exactly gonna be fine."

"She does love you," Connor said, and wished the words didn't sound so weak. CJ only grunted. Connor added, "You'll get through it."

"Yeah." CJ spoke in the affirmative—but he was shaking his head. "I guess I will."

"Tori will be here when your mother comes."

"Why?"

Connor had no idea what his son was thinking. He asked cautiously, "Does that bother you, if Tori's here?"

"No, Dad. It's only…that could be weird."

"Maybe. But Tori says she can handle it. And I think it's a good thing. For your mother to meet my fiancée, to see that we're, all of us, moving on with our lives." His fiancée. So quickly, the lie was getting to be second nature. He kept having to remind himself that it *was* a lie, to draw the line in his mind, between the roles he and Tori played and their real relationship, which was amazing.

But not destined to last.

"Dad?"

"Yeah?"

"You kind of spaced out there for a minute. You okay?"

Connor shook himself. "I'm fine." He got up from the edge of the bed and went to the open door. "Good night."

"Night, Dad."

Tori was up and dressed and ready to go by seven the next morning. She wanted to be able to head for Connor's instantly if his ex should show up before nine.

But the phone didn't ring.

At nine on the dot, she stood at Connor's door. He opened it and pulled her inside before she even had a chance to ring the bell.

He kissed her. One of *those* kisses. The kind that stole her breath and curled her toes and reminded her of all the lovely things he did to her when they were alone in bed.

Eventually, with great reluctance, she pulled away. "Where's CJ?"

"In his room."

"Your ex-wife...?"

"Not here yet. Tea? I think Gerda has some around here somewhere."

"Yes. All right. Tea." Tea would be good. Something to do with her hands—to keep them from reaching for him.

She followed him into the kitchen, which had

everything a gourmet cook might desire: gleaming granite counters, custom cabinets, name-brand stainless-steel appliances. He heated a mug of water in the microwave and stuck a tea bag in it.

"Thank you." She put her hands around the cup, taking comfort from the warmth of it.

There was coffee already made. He was pouring a cup for himself when the doorbell rang.

Connor set the half-filled mug on the counter and put the pot back on the heating pad. "Well. I guess this is it."

Her stomach lurched. But she answered with a smile. "Yes. I think so."

They went back down the central hallway together. She detoured to the living room as they passed it. "I'll wait here. Don't want to overwhelm her at the door." He gave her a nod and continued on to the entry.

Tori perched on a chair in his big, well-furnished living room. She heard the door open, and then a woman's voice—tight, controlled. Connor said something.

And then two sets of footsteps approached.

Connor and a beautiful, very angry-looking blonde appeared in the doorway to the hall. "Jennifer, my fiancée, Tori Jones."

The blonde dismissed her with a look and said to Connor, "Is CJ ready? I want to get going right away."

Tori kept her smile in place as she rose. "It's so great to finally meet you."

Jennifer granted her an icy glance. "Yes, well." And instantly turned back to Connor. "CJ. Where is he?"

Connor shrugged. "In his room."

"Take me to him. Now."

"Sure. This way." Connor sent her a rueful look over his shoulder as he and Jennifer left the doorway.

Tori waited, too nervous to sit back down, until he returned a couple of minutes later.

"Gee," she said when he entered the living room. "That went well."

He let out a heavy sigh. "Sorry. Really."

"Don't be sorry. I volunteered to come, remember? And I still think it's good, that she's met me, that I'm… real to her, you know?"

"Yeah. I guess so."

She frowned. "So…what now?"

"I don't know. We wait, for a few minutes anyway. Give CJ his chance to say what he needs to say."

"What if she tries to drag him out of here?"

Connor actually chuckled. "She's no bigger than he is anymore. And he can be seriously un-draggable when he's made up his mind about something." He took her hand. "Come on. Let's sit down." He led her to the sofa and they sat together.

A tense couple of minutes passed. They held hands; they were quiet, waiting.

And then Tori heard the sound of high heels swiftly, furiously tap-tapping the hardwood floor in the central hallway. The blonde appeared in the doorway again.

"Connor. I told you to have him ready to go. He's not packed. He says he's not going."

"Jennifer, I don't know what more to say to you than I already have. We all agreed he's staying here for the summer and we are keeping that agreement."

Jennifer fumed. Tori could almost see smoke coming out of her delicate, diamond-bedecked ears. "Get him ready. Get him ready now."

Connor let go of Tori's hand and stood. "No, Jennifer. I will do no such thing." Tori rose to stand beside him. A show of solidarity couldn't hurt.

Jennifer looked ready to take Connor's head off with her perfectly manicured hands. "You know what you're asking for, don't you? I will call my lawyers. I'll get a court order. He's going, one way or another."

"I've already called *my* lawyers," Connor said calmly.

"You're bluffing."

"Jennifer. Why would I bluff about such a thing? I called them two hours ago, at nine sharp Eastern time. I told them I'm getting married again and I'll be able to make a fine, supportive family environment for my son. So I'm suing for joint physical custody."

Jennifer's plump red mouth dropped open. "You're not serious."

"Yes, I am. I've also told them about our agreement for this summer and your decision to go back on it. I've explained that CJ wants to stay with me."

"How dare you?"

"I am his father, Jennifer. He's fifteen and his say in this does matter."

"I will have him physically removed from this house."

"No, you won't. My lawyers are aware of your threats and taking steps to block your efforts as we speak."

Jennifer pressed her fingers to her temples, as if suddenly stricken by a really bad headache. "I cannot believe that you're doing this to me."

Tori started to speak, to try to ease the tension a little—though she had the sinking feeling she was completely out of her depth here. That it had been unwise of her to come.

Connor spoke before she did. "I'm not doing this to you, Jennifer. You are not the issue here. CJ is. And I'm doing this for him."

"You are a selfish, selfish man."

"I'm sorry you feel that way." He grabbed for Tori's hand again. Aching for him, she gave it, twining her fingers with his. He said to the blonde in the doorway, "You are more than welcome to see CJ anytime this summer, if you'll simply do us the courtesy of calling in advance. But for now, I think it's best that you go. Please."

"What do you care, you bastard?" she demanded. "You never cared."

Connor didn't defend himself. Which was probably the best choice at that point. "You should go," he said again. "Now."

For maybe thirty seconds, Jennifer stood frozen in place. And then, with a small, enraged sound, she announced, "You will hear from my lawyers."

"Got that. Loud and clear."

Jennifer still refused to go. She hovered there, for an endless moment longer. Tori feared she was going to say something really terrible, something that would finally do it, would serve to break Connor's iron control.

But in the end, she simply whirled on her designer heel and headed for the door. Tori counted it a small blessing that at least she didn't slam it on her way out.

Chapter Ten

Connor sank to the sofa again. Tori sat, too.

He said, his voice stark, barely more than a whisper, "God. She hates me. She's the mother of my son and she hates my guts."

"Connor, don't."

"I thought for a while that she was over all that, that we'd each moved on with our lives. But no. She still hates me."

Tori had kind of figured that out already, but with Jennifer's angry words echoing in her head, the truth became all the more agonizingly clear. She wished she hadn't come—at the same time as she remembered the way he'd grabbed for her hand. As if he needed her, took strength from her presence there.

He seemed to sense the direction of her thoughts.

"I was glad you were here. Just more proof of what a selfish bastard I am."

"You're not, Connor. You're not."

"But I really hate that you had to witness that."

"Not your fault," she reminded him. "It was my idea." She felt she just had to say something in his defense, since he seemed unwilling to do that for himself. "It takes two to make a bad marriage, or at least, that's what I've always believed."

He gave her a rueful glance. "Don't defend me. Please."

"Well, okay. What do I know, anyway? I'm just the fake fiancée."

"You know a lot." His voice was tender. "And as bad as that was, I still think I'm doing the right thing, for CJ."

"Me, too."

There were footsteps in the hallway. CJ appeared and stood in the open doorway where his mother had been. "She's gone?"

Connor replied, "Yeah."

"She was so mad, Dad."

"Yeah. She was."

CJ raked his shaggy hair back off his forehead. He looked very young right then. And there was way too much hurt in the eyes that were so much like his father's. Hurt and determination, too. He stood up straighter. "I think I need to get to work, you know?"

"Good idea," said Connor. "I'll take you now."

CJ gave Tori a shy glance. "See you at two, Ms. Jones."

She sent him a bright smile. "Yes. I'm looking forward to working with you, CJ."

"You could ride along with us," Connor suggested.

Nervously, Tori twisted her engagement ring, caught herself doing it, and made herself stop. "I have lunch at noon with Allaire. And you two might have a few things to talk about. I'll just go back to my place, thanks."

CJ was silent on the drive to the Hopping H. And Connor couldn't think of anything constructive to say then, anyway. Plus, he was worried about Tori.

He never should have allowed her to be there when Jennifer showed up. Tori shouldn't have to deal with crap like that. It wasn't her problem and he feared that the unpleasant encounter had only made her have second thoughts about their temporary engagement.

Halfway to the guest ranch, he knew he was going to race back to Tori's place as soon as CJ got where he needed to go. But then, as he pulled the SUV to a stop in front of the ranch house, he decided that he would leave her alone for the rest of the day.

The woman deserved a little time to herself now and then.

If she changed her mind about everything, so be it. He would certainly understand why.

"Thanks, Dad." CJ got out of the vehicle and ran up the steps to the front door. He went in.

And Melanie came out. She waved at him to wait and then ran to his side window.

He rolled it down.

She made a funny, disbelieving face at him and then accused, "Jerilyn says you and Tori are getting married. Is it true?"

Great. More lies to tell. "Yeah."

"Connor. Since when?"

"Yesterday afternoon. I got down on my knees and begged her. She said yes. We went to Bozeman and bought the ring."

Melanie let out laugh. "Seriously? Really?"

He felt like a jerk for deceiving her. But he continued to do so anyway. "Yeah. Seriously."

She was shaking her head. "You're a fast worker, big brother."

"I see what I want, I go after it."

She reached in the window and patted his shoulder, a fond sort of gesture that made him feel even more like a lying creep. "You certainly do. And I'm happy for you. She's a wonderful person."

"Yes. She is."

"When's the wedding?"

He groaned. "Hold on, will you? We just got engaged."

"All right, I won't push for the details. Yet—and I have an idea."

"Uh-oh."

"Don't be so negative. You haven't even heard what it is."

"No, but I have a feeling you're going to tell me."

"We need a party." She gave a firm nod. "An engagement party. I'll call Allaire. We'll get right on it."

This was getting out of hand. "Hold on. Don't make a big deal. Please."

"Oh, come on. It will be fun. And you and Tori together, engaged to be married, that calls for a celebration. "

"Would you mind if I checked with Tori first? I don't even know if she's told Allaire."

"Of course, she's told Allaire. They're best friends."

"Melanie. I mean it. Wait."

She folded her arms across her middle. "Fine. Talk to Tori. And get back to me. Soon."

"All right. I promise. I'll talk to her."

"How did it go with Jennifer?"

"About as expected. She was furious. She's calling her lawyers. I already called mine."

"It will work out."

"I hope so."

"You did the right thing—and I mean it about the party. Talk to Tori. Get back to me. I'm giving you twenty-four hours on it and then I'm calling Tori myself."

"I can hardly believe it," Allaire said with a combination of wonder and disbelief. "He asked you to marry him and you said yes?"

"That's right. I love him," Tori said simply. She neither choked nor stumbled over the words. And when they came out, they sounded true. Real.

Yes, she'd spent the two and a half hours since leaving Connor's house wondering if she ought to call a halt to this dangerous charade before they got in any deeper.

But then she'd come to the Tottering Teapot for the weekly girls-only lunch and she'd sat across from Allaire at their usual lace-covered table. And she'd made the announcement, simply and directly. With no fanfare.

And no hesitation.

Allaire sat back in her chair. She studied Tori's face for several seconds that seemed like a lifetime and a half. And then, finally, she nodded. And she smiled. "I'm happy for you. And he's a lucky, lucky man."

Tori couldn't help nodding back. "Yes, he is. And I'm a happy woman."

Allaire looked at her sideways. "Ahem. Your left hand."

"Yes?"

"It's under the table."

Tori giggled like a high-school girl. "Yes."

"Come on. Let me see it."

Tori lifted her hand and held it out across table.

"Wow," said Allaire. "Just…wow." She grinned at Tori. "I take back every small-minded thing I ever said about him. That is one gorgeous ring."

"I know. I love it."

Allaire raised her teacup. "To you, my dear friend. And to Connor. And to all the happiness that love can bring."

Tori clinked her cup with her best friend's. They sipped in unison.

Strangely, at that moment, beaming across the table at Allaire, Tori didn't feel like a liar or a cheat.

She felt happy. And hopeful. Like a woman in love.

Connor dropped CJ off at two, as planned. He didn't come in, just waved from the SUV when Tori opened the door.

CJ and Tori worked for the agreed-on two hours. He'd brought his grade reports and several books he and Connor had bookmarked the night before, so he could show her where he was in the classes he'd taken the previous semester.

By the end of the session, Tori felt the tutoring was

going to work out well. CJ seemed seriously committed to getting caught up. And he was a very smart boy. Now he was willing to apply himself, she had little doubt that he would be ready for his junior year when he went back to school in the fall.

At four, as they were finishing up, Jerilyn appeared.

CJ confessed he'd invited her. "I hope that's okay, Ms. Jones…"

She told him it was great and ushered them into the kitchen for snacks and juice. The doorbell rang again.

"That's Dad. He said he'd come get me this time in case I had too many books to carry on my skateboard."

Tori left the kids in the kitchen and went to let him in.

"All finished?" he asked when she pulled open the door.

"We are." Strange how her heart felt lighter, just at the sight of him. "And Jerilyn got here a minute ago, too. Want some juice and crackers?"

He glanced past her shoulder. "Where are they?"

She almost laughed. "In the kitchen—and you're whispering."

"Yeah, well. After this morning, I've been a nervous wreck, waiting to ask you…"

"What?"

"Are we…still on with this?"

"I have to tell you, I did have second thoughts."

He looked stricken. "I knew it."

"But then I went to lunch with Allaire…and told her we're getting married."

Those dark eyes of his were velvet-soft. He

stepped over the threshold and took her by the arms. "Seriously?"

"Seriously." She moved back a step. He came right with her and nudged the door shut behind him.

For a moment, they simply regarded each other. Looking up at him, so close she could feel the heat of his body, seemed to steal all the air from her lungs. And strangely, a thousand butterflies had somehow gotten loose in her stomach.

He lowered his dark head. She raised hers. They shared a kiss as sweet and tender as any kiss could be.

When he lifted his head, he said, "Melanie insists that she's calling Allaire and setting up an engagement party."

She chided, "Don't look so grim. Tell your sister thank you. When people get engaged, the ones they love want to celebrate."

He grumbled. "That's pretty much what Melanie said."

"Shakespeare has a quote for this."

"I know, I know. The one about tangled webs, right?"

"That's it. So I think we should just go for it, you know? We're in this and, unless you want to back out now, Connor, we're staying in it for the next eight weeks or so."

"I don't want to back out—I just keep thinking that *you'll* want to." His voice was gruff.

"Well, stop. I'm not getting cold feet, okay? I agreed to do this and I'm sticking by my agreement. Stop second-guessing me."

He pretended to look chastised. "Yes, Ms. Jones."

"That's better—now come on in the kitchen before the kids come looking for us."

CJ and Jerilyn were at the kitchen table, each with a large glass of orange juice and a plate of organic potato chips.

"Dad, I had a good lesson," CJ announced proudly. "Didn't I, Ms. Jones?"

"We made great progress, yes."

"Dad, can Jerilyn come over for dinner? Afterward, she says she'll help me with my homework—if *her* dad says it's okay, I mean."

"Of course," Connor said. He arched a brow at Tori. "Join us?"

"I'd love to. Yes."

In the sunny summer days that followed, Tori and Connor were together every chance they got. They shared dinners with CJ—at Connor's and at Tori's. Connor would come over to her place in the mornings when CJ was at the Hopping H. And sometimes he also showed up late at night, after his son was in bed. They went out to romantic dinners, once to the resort again, and once into Bozeman to Tori's favorite restaurant there.

Word of their engagement spread fast in Thunder Canyon. There were congratulations on everyone's lips. And each one seemed sincere.

They told his parents and hers. It seemed the wisest course. They didn't want them to hear it from someone else. Her dad and stepmom gave their blessing. His parents didn't sound too thrilled. But at least they were polite in their chilly, distant way.

After they talked to the McFarlanes, Tori teased him

that she now knew of at least two people who wouldn't be the least bit sad to see their engagement come to an end.

Connor grabbed her close and kissed her until her head was spinning. "Don't talk about it ending," he growled. "We've barely begun."

She almost said, *It doesn't have to end, you know.*

But shouldn't he know that? Of course, he did. He cared for her a lot. But he'd made it painfully clear that he didn't intend to marry again. She had to remember that it wasn't forever, that the fantasy they were living was just that. And it was destined to end before the leaves started to fall.

On Thursday, the first of July, a week and three days after Jennifer declared she would sue for full custody, Connor was served with papers from her lawyers. He shrugged and told Tori that Jennifer would be getting his countersuit that same day. She thought he seemed pretty confident.

But then, he always did. He had another meeting with Caleb Douglas that Thursday evening. Caleb's mostly silent partner, Justin Caldwell, showed up that time, too, with his wife, Katie. Justin was Caleb's illegitimate son. And Katie was a close friend of the Douglas family, who had spent several years living in Thunder Canyon as something of an honorary daughter to the Douglases.

Later that night, in her bed, Connor told her that Justin seemed fond of his father and of his half brother, Riley, as well. Connor said Justin wasn't a factor in the sale. Justin was willing to do whatever Caleb decided.

"I got the feeling that he *wasn't* willing to invest any more money, though. And that he'd be happier if Caleb either decided to sell—or found a way to get more investors to put in some green until the economy picks up enough steam that they start seeing real profits again."

She scolded, "Why are you telling me this? Didn't I say I wanted nothing to do with your takeover plans?"

He kissed the tip of her nose. "You *have* nothing to do with them. This is just pillow talk."

"You'd better watch yourself, Mr. Corporate Shark. I'll sell all your secrets to the highest bidder."

He chuckled. "Oh, come on. Corporate spying is not your style."

She pointed at her nose. "These freckles? This school-teacher act? All designed to lull you into trusting me so I can ferret out all of it, learn every trick you have up your sleeve—and pass it on to people who will pay well to know what you're up to."

He bent close, blew in her ear. And then he caught her earlobe between his teeth and bit it just hard enough to make her moan. "I'm in control here."

"Ha. So you think."

He kissed her. Long and deeply.

"Okay," she said when they came up for air. "I see your point."

He kissed her again.

"I forgot." She put on a dazed expression. "What were we talking about?"

And he kissed her a third time.

After that, Tori forgot everything—except the feel of his hands on her body and the touch of his lips to hers.

The next night was Friday, the second of July—and the date of their engagement party.

Melanie and Allaire had managed somehow, on extremely short notice, to get the upstairs ballroom in the town hall on Main Street for the party. This was quite a feat, as it was the weekend of the Fourth with all kinds of community events in the works.

From what Tori heard, practically everybody in town pitched in on the party. They wouldn't let her help. But all day Friday, the ballroom was full of Tori's friends and students—including Jerilyn and CJ, who had gotten a day off from his lessons with Tori so he could help with the party.

Jerilyn came by Tori's house in the late afternoon and reported that they'd spent the day setting up tables and chairs. And decorating. Jerilyn was really proud of the way the decorations had turned out. But she refused to tell Tori anything specific about them.

"Because you should be surprised, Ms. Jones. That's part of the fun."

Tori did know that they were having potluck, with everyone bringing something, to be served buffet-style. And DJ was not only providing condiments and a few side dishes from the Rib Shack, he'd also hired the same six-piece band that would be playing at the Independence Day dance Saturday night. The band didn't mind picking up an extra gig, as long they were in town.

Tori and Connor were given instructions to be there at eight. Not before, not after. Melanie and Russ picked up CJ at six and Jerilyn was getting there with her dad.

Connor, dressed for the occasion in jeans, tooled boots and a gorgeous Western shirt, showed up at Tori's door at seven forty-five. "My sister ordered me to cowboy up for this thing." He didn't look happy. But he sure did look good. Not like a real cowboy—more like a movie star *playing* a cowboy.

She said, "Hey. Works for me."

He came inside and shut the door. "I like that dress. What color is that?"

"Teal blue."

"It matches your eyes."

"My eyes are hazel."

"And right now they look blue-green." The dress was sleeveless, perfect for a summer evening. With a lazy finger, he traced the low, square neckline. "Beautiful."

"Thank you—and why do I get the feeling it's not my dress that interests you?"

Dark eyes gleamed. "Maybe because I'm thinking about what's underneath."

"Don't get ideas. We have to be there at eight sharp."

"I can be quick when I have to."

She gently slapped his hand away. "Uh-uh. I just got ready. You are not messing up my hair—or my makeup."

"I can be careful."

"You are incorrigible."

"So I've been told."

"It's going to be great," she told him. "You'll see." She turned to grab her purse from the entry table. "Now, let's get going."

He scowled. "I think there's some kind of surprise brewing. I don't like surprises."

"Relax. Let all your control issues go, just for one evening. It's going to be fun."

"Control issues?" He arched a dark brow. "I have no control issues."

She wisely refrained from arguing the point.

CJ was waiting on the front steps of the town hall. "I'm supposed to take you up," he said.

Clearly there *was* some kind of surprise brewing.

Connor narrowed his eyes. "What are they plotting?"

CJ wasn't telling. He was trying not to grin. "Come on, Dad. You'll see."

Inside, with CJ in the lead, they mounted the wide, slightly creaky wooden steps that led to a large landing. Wide-open double doors gave way into the hall itself. The lights were off in there—and it seemed much too quiet.

"Come on, you guys." CJ, several steps ahead of them, turned back to signal them onward as he made the landing. But he didn't wait for them. He went on through the doors, vanishing into the large shadowed room beyond.

"I don't like this," Connor muttered out of the corner of his mouth.

She took his hand. "Be brave," she teased.

He grunted but said no more. They reached the landing. Beyond was darkness, punctuated only by the random sparkle of what looked like Mylar streamers hanging from the ceiling. Connor held back.

Tori couldn't suppress a giggle. "This is so exciting."

"Yeah, right."

"Coward," she teased.

"Fine," he grumbled. "Let's get it over with."

Side by side, they stepped into the shadows beyond the doorway.

The lights popped on, blindingly bright, as shouts, applause and catcalls erupted. Simultaneously, the band started playing "Here Comes the Bride," only flat, with a horrible-sounding horn.

And suddenly, an enormous clump of glittery confetti fell from above. For a moment, as the horn played on, they were engulfed in a snowfall of shiny foil and bits of bright paper.

Then everyone came rushing forward to shout congratulations and grab them in bear hugs. That went on for at least five minutes. Tori lost sight of her confetti-covered fake fiancé as each of them was hugged, passed down the line, and hugged again.

Finally, they all seemed to settle down. The band stopped mid-note.

Tori glanced toward the stage at the far end of the hall. Allaire was up there, at the mike, wearing a pretty pink dress, her hair shining like spun gold under the lights, looking like a fairy princess.

"Connor McFarlane," she said. "Congratulations. You are a very fortunate man."

Tori blushed. And everyone started clapping and whistling again.

Allaire raised her hand. "And, Tori, we love you. May you find all the happiness you so richly deserve."

The guests clapped even louder.

Tori shouted, "Thank you. What a great party. Thank you, everyone!"

Tears filled her eyes and guilt tried to creep up on her. All these people, people she cared about, wishing her and Connor well, not knowing it was a lie.

The band struck up a lively tune. The guests dispersed from clogging the doorway, pausing only to clasp Tori's shoulder again, to offer more good wishes. Some coupled up and danced. Others grabbed plates and got in line at the buffet tables.

Connor appeared. "There you are. Lost you there for a minute or two."

She swallowed her tears of guilt and whispered in his ear, "That wasn't so bad, was it?"

He grunted. "Okay, I admit it. It could have been worse."

Laughing, they brushed at each other's shoulders and hair, thinning out the confetti snowfall a little.

CJ and Jerilyn came toward them. Both were grinning wide. CJ called, "Sweet, huh, Dad?"

"Yeah," said Connor dryly. "Sweet."

It seemed to Tori that the whole town was there. The kids from her classes, everyone from school, every Traub and Clifton, every Cates and every Douglas, too.

She and Connor found a table with a couple of free seats. She admired the decorations, which involved flags and Uncle Sam hats and patriotic bunting, everything doused with glitter, in red, white and blue. And the ceiling? A sea of shining Mylar streamers.

Connor went and got them soft drinks—no liquor allowed in the hall. Later, they went through the buffet line, loading up their plates with more than they would ever be able to eat.

They danced. He was an excellent dancer. She filed that information away in her growing store of knowledge about him. Funny, how she felt she could never know enough about him. She could spend the rest of her life learning his ways. His likes. His dislikes. His numerous and considerable abilities. His failings, of which there were more than a few.

There would never be enough time, not even in a whole lifetime, to know everything about him, every secret dream, every favorite thing. And they didn't have a lifetime.

They had only right now.

He brushed his lips to her temple, then tipped up her chin with a finger so that she met his eyes as they swayed through a slow song. "You look…almost sad." His voice was low, for her ears alone.

She made her lips tip up in a smile. "I'm not, really. Not sad—or if I am, it's only a little. Mostly, I'm happy. Happier than I've ever been."

He held her gaze, searched her face. But only for a moment. And then he pulled her close again and they danced on through the rest of that song and the next one, too.

Later, when the band took a break, they returned to their table. Russ and Melanie joined them and a few minutes later, Grant Clifton and his wife, Stephanie, came by. Steph said how happy she was for Connor and Tori. And Grant, looking very proud, announced that they were having their first baby in February.

Russ got up and clapped his lifelong friend on the back. "Now that's good news. Boy or girl?"

"Not a clue," said Grant.

Russ raised his Pepsi. "Here's to baby Clifton."

"To baby Clifton," everyone at the table echoed in unison.

Stephanie laughed and patted her still-flat tummy. "Grant's already trying to get me to take it easy. I tell him to back off. I've got a ranch to run."

Grant wrapped an arm around his wife and pulled her close for a quick kiss. And then Melanie was up and reaching for a hug from Steph. Tori got up, too, to congratulate Steph with a hug of her own.

When Tori took her chair again, Grant was leaning close to Connor, saying something in his ear that the rest of the table couldn't hear.

"Sure," said Connor. "Monday at ten."

Grant nodded. Tori thought he looked way too serious. And worried, as well. "Thanks."

The band started up again. Grant took Steph's hand and led her out onto the floor.

Tori leaned closer to Connor. "What was that about?"

He put his lips to her ear. "Long story. Later."

Tori shrugged and let it go. She sat back and enjoyed the rest of the evening, which went by in a warm blur of good company, music and laughter.

At the end, CJ went back to the ranch with the Chiltons. He seemed happy to go and looking forward to visiting the foals at the Flying J. That left Tori and Connor with a whole night to themselves.

At her house, they agreed that the party had been terrific. And they also agreed that they refused to feel guilty that the whole town had just celebrated an engagement that would never get all the way to the altar. It had been a town event at minimal cost to all involved and everyone had seemed to have a good time.

They made unhurried love.

Later, as they lay side by side in her darkened room, slowly drifting toward sleep, she remembered that strange moment at the table, with Grant. "So..."

"Um?"

"What was that about with Grant tonight?"

He touched her, smoothing a hand down the curve of her thigh. "Do we really need to talk about Grant?"

"Come on." She caught that wandering hand of his, brought it to her lips and then twined her fingers with his. "I do want to know."

He pulled his hand away. "Tori…"

"Come on." She nudged him in the arm with her elbow.

And finally, he gave in and told her. "Grant wants to meet with me. At his office, one-to-one, up at the resort. Monday morning. I'm not looking forward to it."

"Why not?"

"Last time I met with him, he called me a vulture."

"Not Grant."

"Yeah. Grant."

"When was that?"

"Before I left for the trip to Philadelphia."

"You never mentioned that."

"You didn't want to hear about it then, remember?" Tenderly, he guided a strand of hair off her cheek. "That was before you decided to seduce me and steal all my corporate secrets."

"But what happened? Fill me in."

"Not much. He'd been in denial, I guess. And he finally had to admit to himself that I really was likely to end up buying the resort. He didn't like it. And let me know that in no uncertain terms."

"Poor Grant. He loves that resort so much." She canted up on an elbow and peered down at Connor's face through the dimness. "I'm sure he wants to meet with you in order to work things out with you."

"There's nothing to work out."

"Of course there is, if he was out of line."

Connor was silent.

She asked softly, "You'll keep him on, won't you, when you take over?"

His shadowed eyes gave nothing away. "It's still if, not when."

"Oh, please. You can't fool me. And you didn't answer my question. Will you keep Grant on?"

Again, he didn't reply for the longest time. Then, finally, "It's doubtful. For a number of reasons."

"What reasons?" She asked the question a little too heatedly.

"Tori. Look." Suddenly his voice was weary. "Can we not get into a fight over this?"

"I'm not getting in a fight. I just want to know why you can't keep Grant on."

"Because I have to have someone I can work with, not someone who resents me for taking over 'his' baby. Because he's the one who's been in charge while things went from bad to worse."

"It's not his fault that the recession hit. His ideas *and* his follow-through were stellar. And the resort is everything to him. And for crying out loud, his wife's having a baby—"

He hooked a hand around her neck and brought her face down close to his. "Stop." And he kissed her, hard.

She refused to return the kiss. And when he let her go, she flopped over onto her back again.

He lay beside her, unmoving. They were both silent for a long time.

Finally, she spoke again. "I'm sorry. I just hate it, that's all, when things don't work out for good people."

He shifted beside her and pushed back the covers. "I understand." He was on his feet, reaching for his clothes. Leaving, apparently.

She sat up. "Connor, wait."

He had his boxer briefs on, his jeans in his hands. "It's okay. Seriously. I know exactly what you're telling me. I get it. And I'm not angry at you."

"Then why are you going?"

He didn't answer, only shoved his feet into the jeans.

"Stay," she whispered softly.

"No. Not tonight." He sat in the chair in the corner and put on his socks and his boots. Then he grabbed that fancy Western shirt off the back of the chair and stuck his arms in the sleeves.

She still didn't get this. "But I don't—"

"Just let it go." He rose again and buttoned his shirt. "Please."

She realized that he really was leaving and there was nothing she could do or say to make him change his mind.

"Good night," he said softly.

She only nodded. And she closed her eyes as he turned from her so she wouldn't have to watch him go.

He called her when he got back to his house. "I'm sorry I walked out like that. Honestly. And I meant what I said. It's not about you."

"So then why did you go?"

"You think I like firing people? I don't. But it's business and I have to do what's necessary."

She felt absurdly hopeful. "It does bother you, then,

to fire a man even though the only thing he did wrong was to be in charge when the economy went down the tubes?"

"Fine," he confessed low. "Yes, it does bother me. It bothers me more than it used to."

"That's *so* good to hear."

"For you, maybe. From where I'm standing, it's pretty damn scary. In the past, I was tougher. And a man needs to be tough, especially in times like these."

"You're still plenty tough, believe me. Maybe too tough."

"A man can't be too tough."

"Yes, he can. I'm glad it bothers you," she said, with conviction. "It *should* bother you."

"Tori. Look. Can we just leave it at I'm sorry? And I don't think we should talk about the resort anymore."

She reminded herself that he wasn't really her fiancé, that she didn't need to get to the rock-bottom of this issue—or any issue—with him. She didn't need to know all his secrets.

Too bad something in her hungry heart kept driving her to learn them.

But he was right. She could let it go. Just like she would be letting *him* go in August.

"Tori. You still with me?"

She took a long, slow breath. "Right here."

"Good. First thing in the morning, then? Come to my place. I'll cook breakfast."

She thought of the engagement party, how much fun it had been—how somewhere deep in her heart, she wished that celebration could have been real. She wished that her beautiful engagement ring actually meant forever. She wished that *they* were forever, bonded for a lifetime, she and Connor.

But they weren't. And that hurt. It hurt way too much.

Oh, she should have known it would be like this, shouldn't she? Who had she been kidding? The attraction had been much too strong, right from that first night when he took her to dinner at the Gallatin Room. She should have seen this coming, should have know that this would happen.

She swallowed a groan as the revelation came at her.

She was in love with him. In love with Connor.

How could that be? It was impossible. Falling in love with Connor was never the plan.

But somehow, it had happened anyway.

Chapter Eleven

"Tori?" Connor's voice broke through her thoughts.

"Yes. What?"

"Are you all right?"

No. I'm not. Not all right in the least. And what were they talking about?

She remembered. Breakfast. "Yes," she said tightly into the phone. "I'll be there."

"Terrific."

She had to get off the phone, to be alone with her misery. *In love with Connor.* It was impossible. And also true. She schooled her voice to a bland tone. "Eight o'clock?"

"See you then."

And he was gone, just like that. Dead air on the other end of the line. Smart man, not to give her even a second to reconsider.

She should be that smart. Or at least, smart enough not to fall for the local corporate shark. Smart enough not to pretend to be engaged to a man she could never have in any lasting way.

She hung up the phone and pulled the covers close around her. Which was pointless, really. She loved Connor McFarlane. It was a disaster. No way was she going to be able to sleep.

But she did sleep. And soundly, too. The next thing she knew, it was after seven and sunlight streamed in between a space in the curtains.

At eight on the dot, Connor saw her coming up the walk and breathed a sigh of pure relief. He answered the door as she mounted the steps. "You're here."

"I said I would be."

His damn heart felt constricted in his chest. "God. You're so beautiful."

She looked angry, almost. Probably still ticked at him over last night. She said, "If you know what's good for you, you won't say a word about my freckles."

He didn't care if she was angry. She would get over it. He was just so damn glad to see her. He didn't even try to hide his slow grin. "You stopped me just in time." He grabbed her hand and pulled her inside and into his arms where she fit perfectly.

"I don't know if I want to kiss you." She scowled up at him as he lowered his head.

"Kiss me anyway."

She didn't argue further, so he claimed her sweet mouth. It was one of those kisses that made steam come out his ears and had him wanting only to take her straight to bed.

But he'd promised her breakfast. He took her hand and led her to the kitchen. They had omelets and fresh fruit. Coffee for him, tea for her.

And *then* he took her to bed.

Later, they met Russ, Melanie and the boys in town, for the third of July street fair the merchants put together. They all had lunch at the Hitching Post, which had once been the town's most notorious house of ill repute. Now it was a tavern, the neighborhood kind, where the kids could be included.

Connor saw the blonde woman, Erin, the one he'd met at the summer kickoff barbecue. She was sitting with Haley Anderson, who wore the Hitching Post uniform, but appeared to be on a break.

He also spotted Grant Clifton, with his pretty pregnant wife, at a table across the room. Their eyes met. Grant waved, but didn't smile. Connor waved back and thought about the argument with Tori the night before.

He shouldn't have walked out on her, shouldn't have let the things she said get to him so completely. But he really hated the situation, hated that he agreed with her. It sucked to know that he would be a fool to keep Grant on the payroll when the deal was done.

Which was ridiculous. In business, a man did what he had to do. He tried to play fair, but he couldn't afford to let sentimentality take over. He had to be practical, to make the necessary decisions, no matter how ruthless such decisions might seem to others.

Sometimes, lately, Connor wondered what the hell kind of sap he was turning into. Yes, he'd set out to make a few changes in himself, to heal the rift he'd created with his sister, to have a real relationship with his son. To be a better man.

But not too damn much better. It was getting so he hardly knew the man he saw when he looked in the mirror. It was not a comfortable feeling, to be a stranger inside his own skin.

That evening, Tori made dinner at her house for him and for CJ. He took CJ home at a little after eight and he was back at Tori's door at midnight.

"I missed you," he said when she opened the door.

"You've only been gone a few hours," she chided.

"I know," he whispered. "I missed you anyway."

She didn't say anything more, only searched his face with shadowed eyes. Which was probably just as well. He came inside. She shut the door.

And then she took his hand and led him to her bedroom.

Sunday was the Fourth of July. There was an annual parade along Main Street and a rodeo afterward at the fairgrounds. Melanie had them all out to the Hopping H for dinner. Jerilyn and her dad came, too. They got a large table in the dining room. Since every room was booked, all the other tables were full, too.

Connor went to Tori again that night. They made love for hours. And then they must have dropped off to sleep. He woke in the deepest part of the night, alone in the bed.

Groggily, he dragged himself up against the pillow. "Tori?"

"Right here." She materialized out of the shadows as she rose from the corner chair.

"Everything okay?"

She didn't answer right away. Instead, she came to the bed and dropped her lightweight robe from her shoulders. "Everything is fine." Her pretty body tempted him, smooth and curvy. Her skin had an otherworldly glow in the darkness.

He reached for her. She came down to him and kissed him. They made love again.

Afterward, before he left, he held her. She felt perfect in his arms. He never wanted to let her go.

But somehow, he felt that he was losing her. It was, just barely, the fifth of July. They were supposed to have weeks yet.

But he couldn't shake the feeling that it would all be over much sooner than that.

The first thing Grant did Monday morning was to apologize.

"I was wrong to blame you, Connor. It's not your fault that we're in trouble here, not your fault that we can't go on as we have been." He gave a rueful smile. "And, no, I didn't get you up here to try to convince you that I should stay on when you take over. I can see how that would be a bad idea."

Connor offered his hand. "No hard feelings."

Grant took it. "None."

Connor studied the other man's face. "What else?"

"An hour of your time."

"For…?"

"Let me take you around, introduce you to some of the staff."

"I've met a lot of the staff."

"Humor me. Hear my take on things. Can't hurt."

"That's true."

"And you never know. You might see the resort in a whole new light."

Connor almost smiled. "Now you're scaring me."

"Yeah, well. These are scary times. What do you say?"

"Lead the way."

The tour took longer than an hour. It started at the front desk, where Connor met Erika Rodriguez, who was young and pretty, polite and very professional.

"She's a great worker, smart. Efficient. And dependable," Grant said after they moved on. "And she has a toddler she's raising on her own."

"I get it," said Connor. "You want me to keep *her* on, at least."

"Hell. I want you to keep *everyone* on. It's no secret."

"That won't be possible."

Grant's lopsided smile was way too charming. "I know that. But you can't blame a man for trying."

The rest of the tour was more of the same. Connor met housekeepers and bartenders, spa workers and grounds people. Grant made sure he understood why each and every one of them not only needed the job, but deserved to stay on.

After the tour, Grant convinced him to have lunch with him in the Gallatin Room. Nothing had changed there. Both the food and the service were top-notch. By the time Connor left the resort, he and Grant were on good terms.

And he was even more ambivalent. About everything.

The more time he spent at the resort, the more he second-guessed his decision to take it over. Maybe his father, in trying to manipulate Connor into returning early to Philadelphia, had made a valid point, after all: the resort didn't fit the McFarlane House brand.

Until lately, Connor had been going on the theory that this was a good thing, that McFarlane House needed to try something new, to expand on its own template, to re-create itself during the recession. But now he couldn't help thinking that there were more ways than one to effect the change that was needed.

That afternoon, when he went to Tori's, she didn't ask him how the meeting with Grant had gone. He kind of wished she had. He really wanted to talk with her about it.

But he had suggested they not discuss the resort and she was only doing what he had asked of her. He should be happy with that. He *would* be happy with that.

The summer days sped by. He cherished every moment with Tori. Sometimes he noticed a certain reserve in her manner—a certain watchful distance. But when he asked her if anything was wrong, she would smile and tell him there was nothing.

CJ was doing really well with his studies, and he loved his job at the Hopping H. Twice in the week and a half following the engagement party, CJ broached the subject of staying in Thunder Canyon for the school year.

Both times, Connor insisted that was never going to happen—while, at the same time, he was beginning to wonder why CJ *shouldn't* go to school here. CJ loved his life here. He had his aunt and uncle, his cousin. He had *family* here. Going to the best prep school in the country wasn't everything, after all. For a kid to feel part of a community, to feel loved and supported…that mattered, too.

Connor dropped by the Hopping H often to see his sister and share a cup of coffee when she had a spare moment, or to have a beer with Russ. Once, when it was the three of them alone in the Hopping H kitchen, he even brought up the possibility of CJ staying in town for the school term.

Both Melanie and Russ said CJ would be more than welcome to stay with them. That they loved him, and Ryan idolized him. It would be good for Ryan, to have his cousin around.

"It's not going to happen, of course," Connor ended up insisting. "I was just talking hypothetically."

"Well, if it did," his sister said, "we would be absolutely thrilled to have CJ with us whenever he needed a place to stay."

He got a report from his lawyers concerning the custody suit. His countersuit was officially filed, the legal battle set in motion. The process server had found Jennifer in Greece and laid the papers in her hand.

Connor met with Caleb and Riley and Justin Caldwell again. Nothing was decided. But he knew it was time to call in the McFarlane House legal team, time to put the offer together and lay it on the table. His monthly trip to headquarters was coming up the nineteenth. He would set everything in motion then.

And he kept thinking how quickly the end of the summer would be upon him. That CJ would go back to school. That he and Tori would break up, according to the plan. That he would go home to Philadelphia, buy another house…

About there, he would finally stop himself. He would

remind himself for the umpteenth time that it was only mid-July. He had more than a month left—with Tori, and with his son, in Thunder Canyon. He really needed to stop thinking it was over when so much time still remained.

Then, on the fourteenth of July, he got a call from Jennifer.

"I'd like to…meet you with tomorrow," she said in a tone that was troubling in its hesitancy. "Is that possible? Could I come to your house at ten? And could you have CJ there when I arrive?"

All those questions. The strange lack of hostility. What she was up to now?

"Connor," she said when he didn't answer immediately. "Will that work for you?"

It was very short notice. He could have refused.

But why? He didn't want to deny her contact with CJ. Not really. He just wanted the joint physical custody he should have demanded in the first place. He wanted to make certain CJ got the summer he was enjoying so much. Not to mention a father. For too many years, Connor had denied his son a dad. Not anymore. Never again.

"Of course," he said. "Ten a.m. CJ will be here."

As soon as he hung up, he went straight to Tori's house and explained what was happening. He really wasn't going to ask her to be there. It just wasn't right to put that on her, to keep dragging her into it when he had to deal with his ex.

But she said, "I'd be happy to be there—I mean, if that would be helpful to you."

He should have told her it wasn't necessary. That in the end, he would have to deal with Jennifer on his own anyway. But he didn't. "That would be terrific, if you could. Solidarity is a good thing, I think."

She agreed she would be there.

So the next morning, CJ, looking a little grim, stayed home from work to see his mother. And Tori was there with Connor when the doorbell rang.

Connor opened the door to discover Jennifer, dressed to the nines as always, and clutching the arm of her fiancé, Constantin Kronidis. Up until that moment, Connor had never met the man. But he'd seen pictures. Short, powerfully built and in his early fifties, Kronidis had curly black hair streaked with gray and piercing black eyes. He also possessed the considerable magnetism of a man who had made billions and loved living large.

Kronidis stuck out his hand right there at the door. "Connor, hello. I am so pleased to make your acquaintance at last."

Connor managed to hide his surprise at the unexpected appearance of the other man. "Constantin. Good to meet you." He nodded at Jennifer. "Jennifer."

She actually forced a smile. "Connor."

"Come on in…"

CJ and Tori were waiting in the living room. Connor made the introductions. There were handshakes and greetings. Kronidis was courtly to Tori and warm toward CJ. Connor found himself thinking his ex-wife could have done a whole lot worse in her second husband.

"How about some coffee?" Connor offered.

Kronidis turned to Jennifer and she met his dark eyes. Connor, stunned, saw real affection in that shared glance. Kronidis said, "Yes. Coffee. Thank you."

So Connor went to the kitchen and gave Gerda the go-ahead. She had it all ready to serve.

There was polite conversation while the coffee was poured and sweet rolls and muffins offered around. Kronidis had a sip or two, and then he rose.

"Well. I know important issues are to be discussed here. I only wanted to meet you. I felt it was about time." Jennifer stood and they shared a quick kiss. "I shall wait in the car." Connor started to rise. "No. Please. I am perfectly capable of seeing myself out."

Kronidis took his leave.

When the front door shut behind him, Jennifer spoke. "CJ, I wonder if we could have a few minutes alone."

Without a word, CJ rose and followed Jennifer down the hall.

"Well," said Tori softly as soon as they were out of sight, "this isn't what I'd expected."

"I have to agree with you there."

"I wonder...should I stay?"

He looked in those amazing hazel eyes. And knew he should let her go. But when he spoke, it was only to tell her, "I hope you will."

She said no more. He drank his coffee and she nibbled a muffin and they waited for whatever was happening in CJ's room to end.

The next ten minutes or so seemed like forever. But finally, CJ and his mother reentered the room. There was no mistaking the wide smile on CJ's face. Something good had happened.

The only question was what?

They learned soon enough. CJ bounced over and sat in the far chair.

Jennifer sat next to him, across the coffee table from Connor and Tori. "I hope it's all right that I brought Constantin in with me. He really did want to meet you."

"Of course," said Connor, wishing she would hurry up and tell him what the hell was going on here.

"He's…a family man at heart, Constantin. And he has not been pleased with me lately." She had her hands folded neatly in her lap. She glanced down at them, and then, with a slow breath, raised her head and straightened her shoulders. "He said I had to choose, between a life with him and a life battling my ex-husband. He said it wasn't right, for me to try to—"

She paused to swallow. And then continued. "To take CJ away from his father. That we should all be working together, so that everyone can have a better life. He said—" She looked directly at Connor then. And waved a hand. "Well. It doesn't matter what he said, exactly. What matters is that I did listen. I did see that perhaps I've been…bitter. Angry. Thinking of getting back at you rather than doing the right thing."

Connor could hardly believe what he was hearing. Somehow, he managed to keep his expression composed, though he kept wanting to pinch himself. Could vindictive, cold-hearted Jennifer really be saying these reasonable things?

And then Jennifer said, "So I'm going to drop the custody suit. If you will drop your countersuit, I think we can agree to share both legal and physical custody."

It was true. This was really happening. Jennifer, of all people, was changing—and in a good way. "I would be only too happy to do that," he said with a slow nod. "I'll get with my lawyers and tell them that we've come to an agreement on our own."

"That will be fine," she said, sounding relieved. "Have them contact my lawyers. We'll still need to settle it all legally."

"Yes, I know. I'll do that."

Beside her, CJ was beaming.

Jennifer rose. "Well, that's all then." She aimed a careful smile at Tori. "I'm sorry about last time."

"No problem," Tori answered, rising. "Honestly."

"It's lovely to meet you." If she didn't sound exactly sincere, well, at least she was making a good-faith effort. "I hope you and Connor will be...very happy."

"And you and Constantin, too." Tori bestowed one of her most gracious smiles.

Jennifer glanced at CJ. He bounced to his feet and hugged her. Then she turned to Connor. "Walk me out?"

"Of course." Connor got up and followed his ex-wife to the door.

Once it was just the two of them, on the porch, she said quietly, "I wanted to discuss this last issue where CJ couldn't hear."

"All right." *This last issue.* It sounded ominous.

"CJ wants to stay here for the school year."

"Yes." He hurried to reassure her. "I've made it clear that it isn't going to happen."

"He told me he's doing well, studying with Tori?"

"Yes. He's doing very well."

"Then I wouldn't be averse to his staying here to go to school."

If what went before had seemed improbable, what Jennifer had just said was downright incredible. Connor had to consciously stop himself from gaping like a dumbstruck fool. "You're serious?"

"Yes, I am. I would want him with Constantin and me on a regular basis, for at least a few months total in the year. But he's growing up now."

"Uh. Yes, he is."

"He has a right to make a few decisions for himself."

"He, uh, he certainly does."

"Discuss it with him. Call me."

"I will."

Inside, CJ was not only beaming at the way things had turned out, he was also ready to go to work. Tori wanted to go on home. Connor told her he'd be over to see her, as soon as he took CJ to the Hopping H.

On the ride out to Melanie's ranch, Connor told his son what Jennifer had said out on the porch.

CJ knew what he wanted. "Well, Dad, I do want to go to school here." His brown eyes were shining.

So it was settled, except for the thousand and one details. Connor would have to speak with Melanie and Russ again about this, ask them if they'd meant it when they said CJ could stay with them. And CJ's visits with his mother and Constantin would have to be scheduled.

"All right, then," Connor said, as he pulled into the yard at the Hopping H ranch house. "We can work everything else out as we go along."

"You bet we can, Dad. It's all going to turn out fine." CJ sent him a big, warm smile before shoving open his door. "See you at one?"

"I'll be here."

"Dad?"

"Yeah."

"Now and then, even men need a hug."

"Yes, they do." And he leaned awkwardly across the console and hugged his son.

"I love you, Dad," CJ said in a whisper.

"And I love you, son."

Connor drove back to town thinking about miracles. Because somehow, in the past month, the sulky, troubled CJ had disappeared. His son was back on track, and more. He was a happy kid now, working hard at his studies, comfortable in his new hometown. The change was all that Connor might have hoped for—and more.

He thought about Tori. And he wished…

What? That he could ask her to marry him and really mean it this time? That they could have forever, together, after all? Live happily every after in Thunder Canyon, Montana?

That was not going to happen. He lived in Philadelphia. He traveled a lot. His work was his whole life. Tori deserved so much more than he could ever offer her.

Plus, she belonged here. She loved it here. She'd told him once that she planned to live in Thunder Canyon until she was old and gray. He believed that.

And even though he seemed to have made a kind of peace with his ex-wife, he was far from ready to try marriage again. Not even to someone as terrific as Tori.

He made the turn to her house, and felt the eagerness rise in him. To see her. To be with her. To take her in his arms.

No, it wasn't going to last forever. But while it did, he intended to make the most of every moment.

Chapter Twelve

Tori was waiting for Connor to arrive.

She had a few things to say to him. Important things. Difficult things. And her intentions must have been there, written clearly on her face. Because he knew it instantly when she opened the door to him. She watched his expression change from glad—to apprehensive.

"What?" he said. "What's happened?"

She led him into the kitchen, poured him some coffee and slid into the chair across from him. "The custody battle is over. And everybody won."

He looked at the cup in front of him, but didn't touch it. "Yeah. Good news, huh?"

"Good news." She forced a smile.

He added, "And it also looks like CJ will be staying here for the school year."

That surprised her. It was, apparently, a day for surprises. "Wow. When did that happen?"

"When I walked Jennifer outside. She told me it was
time that CJ got to make a few decisions for himself."

"You talked to CJ about it?"

He nodded. "On the way to the Hopping H. He's
excited."

"I'll bet he's floating on air." Did that mean Connor
would be living full-time in Thunder Canyon? Hope
rose within her, but she tamped it down.

He said, "I think Melanie and Russ will take him,
when I'm not around."

"Ah." She should have guessed. She asked carefully,
"Do you...trust that Jennifer will keep her word about
all of this?"

"I do." His answer was firm. "Mostly because of
Constantin. After seeing them together today, I think
he really loves her."

"And she loves him."

"Yes. I think he'll keep her honest."

Her chest felt tight. She drew in a slow breath. "Yeah.
I see that."

"Tori. What's going on?"

She folded her hands on the tabletop. The showy
engagement diamond he'd bought for her caught the
light and glittered brightly. "We started down this road
so CJ could have his summer here. Now we know he
will have the summer—and the school year, too."

His eyes were dark as the middle of the night. "What
are you telling me?"

"That I think it's time we...talked."

"We *are* talking."

"I mean, about us."

"What about us?"

"About how we're going to end this fake engagement of ours."

There was a silence. A bleak one. Tori tried to gauge his response. She couldn't read him.

He took his coffee cup by the handle, but only to move it a few inches to the right. He didn't raise it to his lips. "We already talked about it. In August, we'll tell everyone we broke up."

She looked at him patiently. "Connor. Please. There's no reason to wait for August now."

He did drink then. He lifted the cup, knocked back a gulp, set it down again. "Right now? Is that what you're saying? You want to end it now?"

"No."

"Then what are you getting at?"

"I don't... I think it's time we started stepping back."

"Stepping back." He echoed her words with hollow precision. "And just how do you want to do that?"

"We need to begin to...drift apart. I'll still wear your ring." She twisted the gorgeous thing on her finger, caught herself. Let it go. "But I think we should stop spending so much time together. I think we should stop...sleeping together."

Again, he echoed her. "Stop sleeping together..."

"Yes. I, well, I'd like a little time, you know? I need to separate what's real from the story we made up. And the best way for me to do that is not to, um, make love with you anymore."

"When did you decide this?"

"I've been thinking about it for a while now."

"And yet you kept telling me that everything was fine." It was an accusation.

"Oh, Connor. It was bound to end. We both knew that. I'm only saying I want to get real about this. Now that Jennifer has come around, we don't have to pretend anymore. And I want that, I want to stop pretending, at least when it comes to the two of us, one on one."

"Let me get this straight. You want to break up—to end it now, as far as what we *really* have together." His voice was hard. Flat. "But until the end of August, we'll go on pretending that we're still engaged."

"Or not. That's okay, too. We can end it right now, if that's better for you. I just thought, since you'll be here full-time at least until then, it would be better for you if you didn't have to deal with all the questions, with everyone in town wondering went wrong."

"I don't give a damn what everyone thinks. Now the custody issue is resolved, it's fine, okay? Whatever you want."

She longed for him to understand. But she could see that he didn't. Softly, she chided, "You don't *act* like it's fine."

His face was a cold mask, showing her nothing of the man within. "Well, it is. It's fine."

"I don't want to hurt you. I really don't."

"Did I say I was hurt?"

"No. No, of course, you didn't. I just need…some time, that's all. Time to get over you." Her throat was so dry. She swallowed convulsively. She felt like such a coward, to be dancing around the real issue like this. To be going on about getting over him, about needing time, without once having said the main truth, without putting the scariest words right out there. She babbled on. "I need to be reminded that this engagement is just an act. And I can't do that this way, with us being lovers. I keep…losing track, forgetting where the line is, between what's real and what's not."

His cold expression didn't change. "You've been building up to this for a couple of weeks now, haven't you?"

She couldn't deny it. "Yes. That's true. I have."

"Since that night I woke up and you were sitting in the corner…"

"Oh, Connor." And she edged a little closer to the emotional precipice. "It was a day or two before that, if you want to know the exact date."

"What day?" It was a demand.

"It was the night of the engagement party, the night we argued over your plans to fire Grant."

"Why that night?" He sounded like a lawyer. A lawyer cross-examining her, determined to force her to reveal her deepest secret.

She stared at his beloved face across the table. And she knew she was going to do it, was going to lay her heart wide-open, to tell him the hardest truth.

"Why that night?" he commanded a second time.

She trembled. It was so silly, to be this upset. If he loved her, if he'd changed his mind about the future, if he wanted it to end differently than they'd always planned, he would have said so by now.

At least, if she didn't tell him, she could salvage some pride. "You don't want to know, Connor."

"Yes," he said coldly. "I do." He was so very angry.

But she saw right then that his anger was no more the issue than her pride was. There was so much more going on here than hurt feelings, than mere pride. She saw that she needed to tell him. She needed to say the all-important words.

Tori told the truth. "Because the night we argued about Grant was the night I realized I'm in love with you."

Connor's world seemed to tip on its axis.

Should he have known? Why hadn't he known, why hadn't he realized?

And why the hell did he feel so damn happy, all of a sudden?

There was nothing to be happy about. Love wasn't in the deal. He wasn't…ready for that. He didn't think he would ever be.

The sudden joy vanished as quickly as it had risen, leaving him empty. Drained. And disgusted with himself—for the interrogation he'd just put her through, for being such a complete ass about this.

He had nothing to offer her, no right to make demands of her, to badger her into this corner, to force her to reveal to him what would have been better left alone.

All she'd wanted was what she had every right to ask for. To be free. To be done with this beautiful, impossible lie they were living.

He stood up then, the movement so swift that she gasped in surprise. "Tori, I'm sorry. So damn sorry."

She let out a slow breath. And a sad little laugh escaped her. "Well. Not really the response I was hoping for."

"I don't know what's the matter with me, to treat you so badly, to put you through this…inquisition.

After all you've done for me and for my son. That was unforgivable of me."

"Connor. It's all right. Don't—"

He chopped the air with an impatient hand. "No. It's not all right. You're an amazing woman and I've been the luckiest man alive, to have had these few incredible weeks with you. I...didn't want it to end, that's all. Even though it has to end, even though, after what happened today with Jennifer, it's *time* for it to end."

She sat there, gazing up at him. Her hazel eyes were blue-green again, and deep as oceans. "Connor, if you think you need forgiveness from me, you've got it. But as far as I'm concerned, there's nothing to forgive. It's okay that this was difficult for you, okay if you had to be a little hard on me to get through it. I'm not angry at you. I don't *blame* you. I went into this with my eyes wide-open."

"Well, you should be angry at me. You should hate me."

"No. I shouldn't. And I don't hate you. And, Connor, the only reason this has to be over now is because you aren't willing, you know? You don't want this to go anywhere. And I do. And that's why it's time we parted ways."

What could he say to that? She was a million miles ahead of him. "I know. You're right."

She took off the ring, held it out to him.

No way. "Keep it. Sell it. Whatever. I...I can't take it back, Tori. I couldn't bear that."

Her smile was so soft, so full of womanly understanding. She set the ring on the table. "All right, then."

"About CJ..."

"You'll tell him it didn't work out with us—but of

course, I'll still tutor him, at least until school starts when we will evaluate his progress. Unless you've changed your mind about that?"

"No. It would be great if you would. He'll be here at two, as usual?"

"Yes, that's fine."

There was nothing more to say. "Goodbye, Tori." He turned to go.

"Connor." She spoke to his retreating back.

He halted in midstride, but he didn't turn.

"Thank you," she said.

He whirled on her, furious all over again. What was the matter with her, to speak so gently, to gaze at him through tender eyes, to be so…kind? He didn't deserve her kindness. She should be angry with him. Yet she only stood there watching him, the saddest, sweetest smile on her beautiful face.

"Thank you?" he demanded, his voice low and rough. "How can you say that? What are you talking about?"

A tear slid down her cheek, gleaming bright. "All my first dates," she whispered. "It seemed like a thousand of them. And no man was ever right. The timing was always wrong—oh, once or twice in college, I told myself I was in love. I even *made* love. But it was never right. It was never real. I…I couldn't admit to myself, until now. Until *you,* Connor, that it was me."

He still didn't understand. "Tori, I don't—"

She put up a hand. "I've been so afraid, deep in my heart, you know? Afraid of loving. Of losing it all. The way my dad and I lost everything that mattered when my mom died." Another tear fell. She didn't even try to brush it away. "Somehow, I missed the main lesson. That a person has to take a chance, to accept the risk

of losing, of having to live through the pain and loneliness. Because of you, Connor, *for* you, I took the risk."
A small, trembling laugh escaped her. She shook her head. "I took the risk. And it looks like it's turning out just as I always feared, that I have loved and now I'm losing."

He couldn't bear this. "Tori…"

"Uh-uh. Let me say the rest. Let me tell you that I feel…braver, now, because of loving you. Stronger. I know that I can bear the pain and the loneliness when you're gone. I won't like it. Sometimes I'll cry, missing you. But still, I find, deep in my heart, that I'm glad. So glad to have known you. To have called you my love. You *are* a good man," she said, her words soft and gentle as a benediction. "You can stop punishing yourself, stop blaming yourself for everything that hasn't worked out as you intended it to."

He had no answer for her, nothing more to say. He turned and started walking again.

And that time she made no attempt to stop him. She let him go.

Chapter Thirteen

"Ms. Jones, my dad told me. That you're not engaged to him anymore."

"Yes. It...didn't work out for us."

"I wish it had."

"So do I, CJ."

"But you'll still...be my friend?"

"Yes, I will."

"Still let me stop by for juice, with Jerilyn?"

"Definitely. Anytime. With Jerilyn or even if you're by yourself."

"And my dad said we could keep on with the tutoring, even after today. At least until school starts. That it was okay with you."

"That's right. I think it's important."

"Me, too."

"So we'll keep on."

"That's good."

"I agree. Shall we get to work?"

"Yes, Ms. Jones. Let's get to work."

Somehow, Tori got through the rest of the day. And the long night that followed. Her bed seemed huge and empty without Connor in it, holding her close.

Without the possibility that Connor would ever be in it again.

Friday morning, Allaire called. "How about lunch? DJ took Alex up to the resort with him. I'm a free woman until two. The Teapot?"

Tori almost said no. She felt so sad and lost and weepy. The last thing she needed was to break down in tears in the middle of their favorite restaurant.

Then again, if she had Allaire over to her house, she *knew* she would end up in tears. Maybe telling her friend about the breakup in a public place would provide at least some insurance against an emotional scene.

"Tori? You still there?"

"I'm here. And lunch would be perfect. At the Teapot. Noon?"

"I'll be there. Haley's coming, too. She's jazzed. It's a done deal. She got the storefront for ROOTS."

"Great. I want to hear all about it." More insurance against losing it, if Haley was there.

Allaire was waiting for her, alone, at their favorite table. One look at Tori's face, and her best friend knew something was very wrong.

Tori slid into the chair she always sat in.

Allaire said, "My God. What?"

"Where's Haley?"

"She called and said she would be late. Now what's

the matter with you? Something's happened and I want to know what."

Tori put her left hand on the table.

"What?" Allaire demanded again. Then she looked down at Tori's ringless finger. "Oh, no."

Tori nodded. "Yeah."

Allaire leaned closer. "When? What happened?"

"Yesterday. It...didn't work out, that's all."

The waitress appeared. They ordered their usual.

The minute she left them alone, Allaire put her hand over Tori's. "Oh, I can't believe this. You two are so in love."

Tori almost laughed. But she was afraid, if she did, it would only bring on a river of tears. "Well, I love *him*, at least."

"And he loves you. It's so obvious, Tori. I saw it in his eyes every time he looked at you. And I know that you two will work it out. I feel it. I'm sure of it."

Tori did laugh then. "But...you can't stand him."

"Hey. I have a right to be wrong now and then. I know now I judged him too harshly. I mean, if you're in love with him, how bad can he be?"

"Oh, Allaire..."

"It's going to work out."

"I don't think so." She stared across the table at Allaire. And it came to her. She couldn't go on lying to such a dear friend. "Allaire, I..."

"Tell me. Please. I want to hear."

"Yes. All right. And I want you to know." And then, in a whisper, leaning across the table toward her friend, swiftly and without fanfare, Tori told all.

She had just finished when the waitress approached.

They said nothing as she set their tea and sandwiches before them.

When she finally left again, Allaire said, "You should have told me. I can't believe you didn't tell me."

"Well. Now you know."

"I'm glad, at least, that CJ will get to stay here in town."

"Me, too."

"And I think Connor's a fool to let you go."

"He's… I don't know…" The insistent tears threatened to fall again. She swallowed them back. "I think he has trouble letting himself be happy."

Allaire raised her teacup. "Here's to him coming to his senses. And soon."

"I don't think that's going to happen." Tori raised her own cup and touched it to Allaire's. "But I'll certainly drink to the possibility."

A few minutes later, Haley showed up. She was beaming from ear to ear. ROOTS was going to become a reality at last. They congratulated her on her success and discussed how they would all pitch in to fix up the new ROOTS headquarters in the storefront down the street.

Allaire had Tori over for dinner that night. And Saturday, Melanie called. Connor had told his sister that the engagement was over.

"Are you okay?" Melanie wanted to know.

"I'm getting by," Tori replied.

"Want some company? I'm coming into town in an hour."

Tori started to say no, that it wouldn't be a good idea.

But she liked Melanie. And she wouldn't mind a little company—in fact, she'd appreciate some.

Melanie came over. She confessed that Connor had told her everything. "I love my brother," she said with a rueful sigh. "But I told him he's messing up royally, to even consider letting you go."

"Melanie, the engagement was never real. You know that. You said he explained it to you."

Melanie made a low sound in her throat. "Of course it was real. Everyone saw it. You two were meant to be together."

"But we're not together. And we're not going to be."

"That's what I thought about Russ and me. And look at us now."

"I don't see the parallel. You and Russ are nothing like Connor and me."

"Yes, we are. Russ and I married for all kinds of convenient reasons, not one of them love. Or so we thought."

That was hard to believe. "You're not serious. Not you and Russ—"

"Yes, I am. He wanted the Hopping H and I needed help making the guest ranch work. It was a strictly business arrangement. Or so we told ourselves at the time."

Tori couldn't afford to get her hopes up. "It's not the same."

Melanie only smiled at her and said gently, "Love matters. When there's love, all kinds of impossible dreams end up coming true."

Tori nodded. She agreed with Connor's sister. At least, she did in theory. As she had told Connor the

day it ended, she believed that love—that having loved
him—was worth the pain.

But right now, well, she was suffering through the
worst of it. It wasn't easy. It hurt a lot. Sometimes, she
forgot that love was worth it. Sometimes, she thought
that impossible dreams were simply that—impossible.

Sometimes she almost wished she'd never loved him
at all.

Connor had the monthly meetings in Philadelphia
starting Monday.

He gave Gerda four days off, since CJ wanted to stay
with the Chiltons, and he flew out early Sunday. He had
dinner with his parents that evening.

They asked after Tori. He said she was fine.

Yes, he should have gone ahead and told them that
the engagement was off. But he couldn't bear to do it,
couldn't stand to see that cool flare of satisfaction in his
mother's eyes. Couldn't sit there and listen to his father
tell him how it was all for the best. That the schoolteacher from Montana was not the right woman for him
and they were glad he had realized it before he got in
too deep.

In too deep.

He was already there. Deep and going deeper. He
missed her. He missed her really bad.

And his own sister had told him he was an idiot.
Melanie had said she didn't care if he thought he'd gotten engaged to Tori just to improve his chances of getting custody of his son. "Wake up, Connor. You're in
love with Tori Jones. If you know what's good for you,
you'll go and tell her so, right now."

Of course, he hadn't. He wasn't going back to Tori. He wasn't ready for any of that. Not ready for love.

Or so he kept telling himself. Constantly. Over and over.

As if maybe, when he'd said it enough times, he would actually believe it. He would be able to forget her, to get on with his life.

Monday was one meeting after another.

Tuesday, he gave his presentation on the Thunder Canyon Resort buyout. He shocked the hell out of all them at that meeting.

His father looked like he might have a coronary when Connor said, "I want to invest in the resort instead of buying them out. My prospectus is in front of you. When you've had time to study my new plan, I think you'll see that the numbers are solid. We'll leave the current management team in place, and I project we can see a profit from our investment within the next two years. They need capital. We can give it to them. And then share in the returns."

His father sputtered. "But it won't be a McFarlane House project."

"No. It will be a McFarlane House *investment*. I'll look elsewhere for our next project. As you've mentioned more than once, Donovan, the resort doesn't really fit our brand. But the Thunder Canyon Resort can be profitable again. And that means we will profit, too."

There were hours of arguments, of objections and retrenchments.

But Connor refused to back down. In the end, he convinced them all. Even his father couldn't argue with the numbers Connor had provided. And besides, Donovan had never liked the idea of a sprawling ski resort bearing the McFarlane House name.

Connor stayed over that night. He had dinner with his parents again. Donovan was anxious for him to move back home, to get to work on the next acquisition. They did need to start growing the business again, though more cautiously than before.

His mother said, "And of course, we are looking forward to meeting this fiancée of yours."

He put them off. On all fronts.

And he flew back to Montana first thing Wednesday morning.

Thursday, he called Caleb and set up a meeting for that night, at the Douglas Ranch. He asked that Grant and Riley both be there. And Justin Caldwell, too, if possible.

Caleb said they would all be there. And he was as good as his word.

After dessert was served, Connor told them of the offer he was planning to make, that he would invest McFarlane House capital and work with them to get the resort in the black again and to build the Thunder Canyon brand. That the management team would stay the same. "If that's acceptable," he said, "we can go ahead and call the lawyers, put a formal contract together."

When he finished speaking, Caleb rose from his place at the head of the table. "Adele, let's break out the bubbly. It looks to me like we've got ourselves a deal here."

There was agreement all around. Champagne flowed and toasts were offered.

Later, Grant took Connor aside and shook his hand. "It's a fine thing you did, Connor."

"It's a good investment. We're all going to benefit."

"You're a good man."

"Well. Not everybody thinks so."

"Whoever 'not everybody' is, they're full of crap. I liked you from the first. Yeah, I had my doubts there for a while. I made no secret of them. But my first impression was the right one. I'm looking forward to working with you. And to calling you a friend."

The next morning, Connor got in touch with Frank Cates, who with his son Matt owned Cates Construction. He told Frank he was going to need a new house. Yes, the house would be vacant several months out of the year. But when he could be there, he wanted CJ to have a place to call home.

Frank said to come on down to the office. "And bring that pretty schoolteacher of yours with you. You know she's gonna want her say. A woman always does."

Connor opened his mouth to tell Frank that Tori wouldn't be with him, that she was no longer his fiancée. But the words refused to take form. He thanked Frank, set an appointment for Monday and hung up the phone.

"You okay, Mr. M?" Gerda stopped rolling out pie dough long enough to send him a worried look.

He realized he'd been sitting there at the kitchen counter, staring blindly into space for a minute or two, at least. "Uh. Yes, Gerda. Fine. Just fine."

"I have to tell you, you've looked better." She went back to rolling her pie dough. "Men," she muttered under her breath. "Some of 'em got no idea what's best for 'em."

Connor pretended not to hear her as he watched her

expertly lift the flattened crust and lay it into a pie pan. Swiftly and cleanly, she pinched the edges so they were attractively fluted.

She glanced up again. "Get on with you, now. Go see that sweet Ms. J and tell her you can't live without her."

If he'd been his father, he would have fired her on the spot. Or at the very least informed her that his activities were none of her affair and she would be wise to remember that.

But he wasn't his father.

He wasn't even really himself anymore—or not the hard-charging corporate shark he had once been, anyway. Somehow, he'd become someone altogether different.

Someone who actually spent time with his son. Someone who had healed the lifelong breach with his sister. Someone Gerda felt she could lecture. Someone Grant Clifton called a friend.

He jumped up from the counter stool. "I have to go out."

"About time," Gerda grumbled.

He hardly heard her. He was already halfway down the hall.

When Tori opened the door, the sight of her stole the breath from his body. In bare feet, old jeans and a Thunder Canyon High T-shirt, she was the most beautiful woman he had ever beheld.

"Connor?" She said his name disbelievingly. Her hazel eyes were blue-green as oceans again. And suddenly, he wasn't sure what to say.

"I'm not buying out the resort. I'm investing in it. And Grant Clifton says he's proud to be my friend."

"Oh, Connor..." She swiped at those gorgeous wet eyes. And her sweet mouth was trembling.

"I called Frank Cates. He's going to build me a house."

"A house. Of course. How wonderful."

"Frank said to come down to the office. And to bring you. That you would want to have input, that women always do. I didn't tell him that we weren't together anymore. I couldn't bear to say it. And I didn't tell my parents it was over, either. I couldn't bring myself to do that, to tell them we had ended it."

She searched his face. "Connor. Come in. Please. Come in."

He stumbled forward.

She shut the door, then turned and leaned against it, as if her legs were too shaky to hold her up. She whispered, "What are telling me?"

"I..." There was so much to say. Where in hell should he start? "I...know you love this town, that you want to live the rest of your life here."

She put her hand to her throat. "But, Connor, wh-what are you *telling* me?"

"Oh, Tori. I'm, uh, I..." Words had completely deserted him.

But she knew. She understood. "It's happening, isn't it? You and me, it's going to happen. It's going to be okay."

Wordlessly, he nodded.

She whispered, "I have to tell you, I did doubt you. I doubted all of it, all I thought I had learned, doubted you would ever come back, wondered if love was worth it, after all."

He cleared his throat and somehow found his voice.

"And why wouldn't you doubt? Why wouldn't you wonder? I've been such a fool."

She laughed then, a joyous sound. "Oh, yes, you have." And then a small sob escaped her. She drew in a ragged breath. "As to the question you were trying to ask me, I do love it here in Thunder Canyon. But I can be…flexible. When I said I'd never leave, well, that was before I fell in love with you. Love changes people. Love…opens us up to new possibilities."

"New possibilities."

"Oh, Connor. Yes."

"We could…play it by ear then, as far as where we live?"

"We could. Absolutely. I'd be open to that."

He took her hand. "Tori."

"Yes, Connor. Yes."

And he went down on one knee. She made a soft, surprised sound when he did that.

He said, "You have to have your story."

"Yes," she said wonderingly.

"Your proposal story."

"I do. Oh, yes, I do."

"Tori, you've been telling me for weeks that a man *can* change. That I'm a *good* man. Well, I *have* changed. And the man I am now is more than ready. For love. For marriage. For *you*, Tori. Because I love you. And I'm so sorry I didn't admit it to myself and to you earlier, that I caused you pain."

She looked down at him reproachfully. "It's true. You did hurt me. You hurt me terribly."

"I hope you can find it in your heart to forgive me."

And she sighed. "Oh, Connor. Yes. Always. Yes."

"I don't have a ring yet."

She laughed again. "I still have my ring. Did you imagine I wouldn't? I was keeping it. I would have always kept it. Whether you ever came to your senses or not."

"Well, okay. Now would be the time to go and get it."

"I will. In a minute."

"Marry me, Tori."

"Yes, Connor. I will."

He stared up at her, hardly daring to believe that she would really be his. His wife. His lover. His best friend for life.

"Connor."

"Yes?"

She tugged on his hand. "Come up here. Take me in your arms."

He didn't have to be told twice. He swept to his feet and pulled her close. "I love you. Did I say that?"

"You did. But that's okay. You can say it again. You can say it over and over. 'I love you' never gets old."

"I love you, Tori Jones."

"I love *you*, Connor McFarlane."

He kissed her then. A long, deep, thorough kiss. A kiss that promised her everything. His love, his devotion, his absolute commitment to her and the future that would be theirs, together.

"We're getting married," he said in a voice full of wonder. "We're *really* getting married."

She nodded. And then she kissed him again. And then she led him to her bedroom, where she took the ring from a secret compartment of her jewelry box. She gave it to him. And he slid it onto her ring finger where it belonged.

And then he took her in his arms again. He kissed her some more. With love.

And with wonder, too.

A month ago, if someone had dared to tell him this would happen, he would have called that person deluded, misinformed, a silly, romantic fool.

But it *had* happened. Connor had found true love. Their sham engagement had turned real. He would have the life he had finally learned he truly wanted: a life with Tori at his side.

Did it get any better than this? He didn't see how.

But then he gazed down into Tori's shining eyes. And he realized it just might.

Because they had each other. They had love. And with love, anything was possible.

* * * * *

*Don't miss the next book in the new
Special Edition continuity,*
MONTANA MAVERICKS:
THUNDER CANYON COWBOYS
Haley Anderson had a huge crush on
Marlon Cates in high school—and a lasting memory
of one passionate embrace. But tragedy made her
grow up fast, and she's long since gotten over the
footloose cowboy. Until Marlon returns to town,
determined to prove that he's a changed man…

Look for
TAMING THE MONTANA MILLIONAIRE
*by Teresa Southwick
On sale August 2010,
wherever Silhouette Books are sold.*

Silhouette®

COMING NEXT MONTH

Available July 27, 2010

SPECIAL EDITION™

SSECNM0710

REQUEST YOUR FREE BOOKS!

2 FREE NOVELS PLUS 2 FREE GIFTS!

SPECIAL EDITION
Life, Love and Family!

YES! Please send me 2 FREE Silhouette® Special Edition® novels and my 2 FREE gifts (gifts are worth about $10). After receiving them, if I don't wish to receive any more books, I can return the shipping statement marked "cancel." If I don't cancel, I will receive 6 brand-new novels every month and be billed just $4.24 per book in the U.S. or $4.99 per book in Canada. That's a saving of 15% off the cover price! It's quite a bargain! Shipping and handling is just 50¢ per book.* I understand that accepting the 2 free books and gifts places me under no obligation to buy anything. I can always return a shipment and cancel at any time. Even if I never buy another book from Silhouette, the two free books and gifts are mine to keep forever.

235/335 SDN E5RG

Name   (PLEASE PRINT)

Address   Apt. #

City   State/Prov.   Zip/Postal Code

Signature (if under 18, a parent or guardian must sign)

Mail to the **Silhouette Reader Service:**
IN U.S.A.: P.O. Box 1867, Buffalo, NY 14240-1867
IN CANADA: P.O. Box 609, Fort Erie, Ontario L2A 5X3

Not valid for current subscribers to Silhouette Special Edition books.

Want to try two free books from another line?
Call 1-800-873-8635 or visit www.morefreebooks.com.

* Terms and prices subject to change without notice. Prices do not include applicable taxes. N.Y. residents add applicable sales tax. Canadian residents will be charged applicable provincial taxes and GST. Offer not valid in Quebec. This offer is limited to one order per household. All orders subject to approval. Credit or debit balances in a customer's account(s) may be offset by any other outstanding balance owed by or to the customer. Please allow 4 to 6 weeks for delivery. Offer available while quantities last.

Your Privacy: Silhouette is committed to protecting your privacy. Our Privacy Policy is available online at www.eHarlequin.com or upon request from the Reader Service. From time to time we make our lists of customers available to reputable third parties who may have a product or service of interest to you. If you would prefer we not share your name and address, please check here. ☐

Help us get it right—We strive for accurate, respectful and relevant communications. To clarify or modify your communication preferences, visit us at www.ReaderService.com/consumerschoice.

SSE10R

HARLEQUIN®

A *Romance*

FOR EVERY MOOD™

Spotlight on

— Heart & Home —

Heartwarming romances
where love can happen
right when you least expect it.

See the next page to enjoy a sneak peek
from Harlequin® American Romance®,
a Heart and Home series.

*Five hunky Texas single fathers—five stories from
Cathy Gillen Thacker's* LONE STAR DADS *miniseries.
Here's an excerpt from the latest, THE MOMMY PROPOSAL
from Harlequin American Romance.*

"I hear you work miracles," Nate Hutchinson drawled.
Brooke Mitchell had just stepped into his lavishly appointed
office in downtown Fort Worth, Texas.

"Sometimes, I do." Brooke smiled and took the sexy
financier's hand in hers, shook it briefly.

"Good." Nate looked her straight in the eye. "Because
I'm in need of a home makeover—fast. The son of an old
friend is coming to live with me."

She was still tingling from the feel of his warm palm.
"Temporarily or permanently?"

"If all goes according to plan, I'll adopt Landry by
summer's end."

Brooke had heard the founder of Nate Hutchinson
Financial Services was eligible, wealthy and generous to a
fault. She hadn't known he was in the market for a family,
but she supposed she shouldn't be surprised. But Brooke
had figured a man as successful and handsome as Nate
would want one the old-fashioned way. *Not that this was
any of her business...*

"So what's the child like?" she asked crisply, trying not
to think how the marine-blue of Nate's dress shirt deepened
the hue of his eyes.

"I don't know." Nate took a seat behind his massive
antique mahogany desk. He relaxed against the smooth
leather of the chair. "I've never met him."

"Yet you've invited this kid to live with you permanently?"

"It's complicated. But I'm sure it's going to be fine."

Obviously Nate Hutchinson knew as little about teenage

boys as he did about decorating. But that wasn't her problem.
Finding a way to do the assignment without getting the least
bit emotionally involved was.

Find out how a young boy brings Nate and Brooke
together in THE MOMMY PROPOSAL,
coming August 2010 from Harlequin American Romance.

The Balfour Brides

A powerful dynasty,
eight daughters in disgrace...

Absolute scandal has rocked the core of the infamous Balfour family. The glittering, gorgeous daughters are in disgrace.... Banished from the Balfour mansion, they're sent to the boldest, most magnificent men to be wedded, bedded...and tamed!

And so begins a scandalous saga of dazzling glamour and passionate surrender.

8 volumes to collect and treasure!